WHAT HIDES IN THE SHADOWS

REAPERVERSE
BOOK ONE

NIKKI ROBB

KINDLE DIRECT PUBLISHING

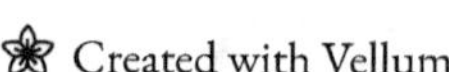 Created with Vellum

For anyone who's ever wished a CW show was a book—this one's for you.

And to Zann and the gaming group, for constantly inspiring me, creating such visceral, monstrous characters, and for always keeping it feral.

CONTENT WARNINGS

What Hides in the Shadows is a New Adult book with fantasy, paranormal, and sci-fi elements. This book contains and alludes to topics such as explicit sexual scenes, drug use (including descriptions of overdoses), being sick (throwing up), suicide, dub-con, cyber-bullying, sexual harassment, and depictions of abusive relationships. Readers who are sensitive to any of these topics please be aware.

Disclaimer: While this story takes place in a real town, all characters and situations are entirely fictional and any similarities to real life instances are purely coincidental.

REAPERVERSE PLAYLIST

Monster- STARSET
90 Days- Pink feat. Wrabel
Monster- Skillet
Call Your Girlfriend- Robyn
I Can See You (Taylor's Version) (From the Vault)- Taylor Swift
We Are Broken- Paramore
Popular Monster- Falling in Reverse
Game of Survival- Ruelle
The Fear of Letting Go- Ruelle
Gravity- A Perfect Circle
Not an Addict- K's Choice
Seven Devils- Florence and the Machine
Heavy in Your Arms- Florence and the Machine
The Handler- Muse
Way Out of Here- Porcupine Tree
Telekenetic- STARSET

THE SECRET SIDE OF ME

My name is Kieran Andras, and I should be dead.

Some people might say that I'm just your average eighteen-year-old kid. I waste my weekdays at Cactus Shadows High School, go to the Friday night football games, dodge my homework deadlines, and have a secret romance like any good textbook teenager would. But with me, that's about where the "averageness" ends.

When I emancipated myself from my parents at fifteen, some people said I was making a mistake. They told me I'd have to grow up too fast, that no one my age should have that kind of weight on their shoulders. What they didn't know was that I'd been weighed down since I called the police for my parents' first overdose when I was five. A kid learns to grow up pretty quickly after something like that. Since then, I'd learned the ropes of surviving addicts, from the threats of drug dealers, to the chaos, and violent outbursts. My "play dates" were with other kids whose parents were just as strung out as mine, where our favorite game was, "Who's gonna call 911 this time?"

In those first few weeks after my emancipation, I felt more

1

like a kid than I ever had before. For once, I was free. But freedom had its price, and I didn't know how to escape who I'd become.

My sophomore year was a blur of monotony and bad decisions. I'd wake up at 3:30 a.m. on the mattress in my crappy studio apartment, no box spring, just the floor, and throw on tight black jeans, a fitted white tee, and my battered leather jacket. A quick run of my fingers through my messy obsidian hair, longer on top, shaved on the sides, followed by a line of coke or something stronger, and I was out the door.

Mornings were spent slogging through a four-hour shift at the gas station before heading to school. Lunch meant meeting Bryce under the bleachers to restock my stash. The afternoons were a haze of ignoring teachers and classmates from the back of the room. After school, it was another shift at the station, then home to get high and start the cycle over again.

It wasn't fulfilling, but it was familiar. And I indulged in it.

Some people assume that after witnessing the damage drugs can do, I'd stay far away from them. But habits are hard to shake, and in my case, chaos was familiar, almost comforting. Turning away from it would have meant leaving behind the only world I really knew.

Every day, the routine repeated itself. Work, get high, school, get high, work, get high. I kept telling myself I was in control, that I could stop anytime I wanted... until I couldn't. Until I caught myself slipping down the same dark tunnel I'd watched my parents disappear into night after night. But instead of clawing my way out, I let go, surrendering completely to the release each hit brought. That tunnel turned into an escalator, one that only went down, and even if I'd wanted to climb back up, I couldn't. Truth was, I didn't want to. The high numbed the pain, dulled the ache of knowing my parents wanted this feeling more than they'd ever wanted me. No matter how hard I tried to escape their ghosts, they were always there, hovering.

Each hit became less about the rush and more about the emptiness it kept at bay.

Then one night, it nearly claimed me for good. I found myself on the edge, the same edge I'd pulled my parents back from more times than I could count. But this time, I was alone. There was no one to steady me, no one to call, no one left to save me as my strength gave way.

Then *he* came.

My Angel.

Echoing in the darkest corners of my mind, his voice called to me, soft and magnetic. He promised me that there was more to life than the numbness I was sinking into, that he could show me a way out, if only I'd trust him. An Angel, here to save me, here to protect me. His tempting voice whispered promises of stability, of companionship...of purpose. It was an offer I couldn't refuse, a lifeline I was desperate to grab ahold of.

So I did.

And I never looked back.

1 FEEL LIKE A MONSTER

It had been just over a year since my Angel saved my life and I sat casually in the back row of my senior year homeroom class, my hands idly fidgeting with a small token in my hand. My fingers grazed the embossed words that read, 'One Year.' My black leather jacket hung over the back of my chair, leaving my tattooed arms bare beneath a fitted white t-shirt. Black inked designs snaked from the collar of my shirt, curving up the side of my neck and flowing down my right arm, ending just below my elbow. Not many students had tattoos, let alone ones that stood out like mine. But then again, not many seniors were emancipated and could sign on their own accord. Plus, the tattoo artist I used was one of Bryce's clients so he always gave me a great deal.

I felt some interested eyes scan my form. I was not oblivious to the attention I received from others, I just didn't care. The only attention I really wanted was some that I knew I'd never get. At least not publicly. And I was ok with that, for now.

Cactus Shadows High School was filled to the brim with the stereotypes that would make John Hughes himself proud.

The petty mean girls, the closeted jocks, the cool kids, the stoners, and the loners. Carefree, Arizona was a dry barren wasteland, but hey, it was home.

The walls of my homeroom were plastered with inspirational posters featuring smiling stock photos and slogans like *"Keep Going," "You Can Do It,"* and *"Success Begins with You."* But the real eyesore was the wall of educational sex-ed posters. The *"Stay Safe, Use Protection"* poster was probably my favorite, purely for entertainment. The glossy photo made teen parenthood look like a horror film, with young parents holding a screaming baby at arm's length as if this was the worst thing to ever happen to them.

I couldn't even argue with it. I knew firsthand what it was like to be the kid nobody wanted, born to the type of people who should have had to pass some kind of test before they were allowed to take a kid home. My parents had me at sixteen, they were those teens who went to football games but didn't see a single play, because they were too busy smoking, or getting handsy under the bleachers. They liked to joke I'd been conceived during the Falcons' worst loss of the season. Pretty fitting, considering the life I ended up with.

Almost as if he appeared to prove my point, Mr. Olsen, the gym teacher and football coach turned health teacher, strolled into the small sterile and poster-plastered room. He wore a grey polo with the Cactus Shadows High logo on the pocket tucked into blue gym shorts. You know the type. The guy whose life peaked when he was on his high school's football team and so he made it his whole personality. And now that his 'glory' days were behind him, he's devoted his life to living vicariously through his athletes. And since coaching doesn't pay the bills, he's taken on teaching health, despite knowing exactly zero about it. Any class taught by the gym teacher was bound to be a blow-off and Mr. Olsen ensured that this class was no exception. His tired blue eyes were framed by grey overgrown eyebrows that matched his salt and pepper short hair.

"Good morning, class." His gruff voice filled the small room easily. A few students shifted quietly in their seats, but other than that he received no response. "Glad to see you're having as good a Monday as I am." He chuckled briefly at his own joke before taking a seat at the desk in the front of the room.

"Mr. Olsen. I just wanted to say congratulations about your team's win this weekend," the blonde from the first row cooed in a low and sultry voice. "It was one hell of a game."

Salem Bridges.

Some people in the school referred to her as 'the girl next door' but I didn't think that title was nearly X rated enough to describe Ms. Bridges. Pretty sure she was on a quest to see how many teachers she could turn on in the middle of class. And from what I have seen, she's got quite a few ticked off the list already. I watched Olsen's reaction carefully, studying his body language. I felt a small smile creep onto my face for the first time in a while. Apparently, I enjoyed the prospect of making our teachers uncomfortable.

Me? With a particular distaste for authority figures? I wonder why.

"Thank you, Ms. Bridges." He spoke with a clear tone, with his eyes trained on Salem.

"Of course...Mr. Olsen." From my vantage point, I could see Salem twirling a piece of her golden hair between her fingers. I could only imagine what her face looked like. Her large brown eyes were probably begging for attention. Her soft lips curved slightly upwards in a smile, with her bottom lip caught between her teeth. I pushed the thought of her lips away. I wasn't about to let my frustrations with my current partner turn into some awkward mess in Health class.

I quickly straightened up and turned my focus back to Mr. Olsen. He nodded a little sheepishly, then scooted his rolling chair a little too close to the desk. Probably a smart move, considering those gym shorts of his didn't exactly leave much to the imagination.

Point for Salem.

I let out a small laugh and leaned back in my chair.

"Do you think they've done it?" The solidly built, six-foot-four-inch mound of muscle with sandy blonde shaggy hair leaned across the aisle and whispered. His everything bagel breath seeping into my personal space was enough to make me gag.

"First, Please stop eating those things and then speaking to me, we've talked about this."

Jace shrugged and grabbed a stick of Doublemint gum from his blue letterman jacket's pocket and popped it into his mouth. "And second, Salem's got much too high of standards for that."

Jace seemed satisfied with my answer, leaning in his chair and tipping it precariously on the back two legs. He'd already fallen twice this year, but Jace wasn't the sharpest tool in the shed. Not exactly the type to learn from his mistakes. I smirked at my friend, though I really hesitated to call him that. That wasn't exactly what we were to each other. What do you even call your former drug dealer's younger brother and protegé who got pissed when you cleaned up and stopped paying him, so you ended up becoming a kind of middleman, directing new kids his way to help him make his monthly quota? *Friend* was the simplest label, but it didn't quite capture the nuances of it all.

"Got any more for me?" Jace asked, his voice eager. No,

eager wasn't the right word- *afraid* was more like it. Jace worked for his older brother, Bryce, who was now a freshman at the local community college. A real hard-ass. I'd worked with Bryce for a while when I was using, and that wasn't a chapter I looked back on fondly.

Jace didn't deal the hard stuff, the kind I used to get from Bryce. The kind I relied on when I was deep in. For anything heavy, I went straight to him. He didn't cut me much slack either, practically forcing me to deal for him to pay my debts, but I needed it, so I played along. Bryce had pulled Jace into the game a while ago, and now he was stuck working under him, bringing in a quota every month or facing Bryce's ruthlessness. I didn't deal anymore, not since I got clean. Not since my Angel saved me.

But here I was, still at the sidelines of this twisted game. I'm pretty sure I always would be.

I think there's only one way out of this game for good, and it's not by winning.

"Not since you texted me this morning."

"Shit, sorry. I know I've been bugging you. But like, I'm like $100 short this month." His eyes darted around. Mr. Olsen droned on in the background about the dangers of addiction and the irony was not lost on me. I was just about to tell Jace to do his own damn job when the classroom phone rang.

"Yello." Mr. Olsen listened in to whoever was on the other end then rolled his eyes before hanging up. "I have to head to the office. Please read chapter two and fill out the answers in the back of the section. I'll be back shortly." Then he sauntered out of the room. It only took a few moments for the class to settle into a low murmur of gossip.

"Have ya all heard about the party t'is weekend?" The

thick Irish accent stuck out among the other low voices in the room. "After the prom. Should be good craic, will it?"

"It's not prom, it's called Homecoming, you dumb brit." Randy, the throwaway jock, laughed with his friends at his own joke. Callum, the Irish exchange student with curly short black hair and tanned skin smiled politely at Randy and stood, offering me a full view of his outfit. Dark jeans and a button-down shirt with the top three buttons open.

"I'm 'fraid you're mistaken, Randy. T'ough I suppose that's to be expected, seeing as you're quite possibly *the* quintessential jock from which every dumb jock stereotype was born."

It was at that moment I realized that *every* insult sounded better in an Irish accent. The class apparently agreed, erupting into laughter that echoed off the walls. Even the other jocks joined in.

If anyone else had said that, they'd probably be picking their teeth up off the floor right now. But instead, Randy's crew were laughing right along with everyone else.

It had to be the accent.

"I'm not 'a Brit'. I'm Irish, ya bellend," Callum finished, sitting back down with an air of superiority, and finality.

There was a pretty widespread rumor going around that his accent was fake and that he's actually just some theatre kid from Wisconsin who's really into dialects. I'd hate to be him if that was ever proven true. High school can be ruthless. Especially to anyone deemed 'different' or 'weird.' I hoped for his sake that he was as Irish as a four leaf clover, or whatever else isn't an offensive Irish stereotype.

The class settled back into their dull drone of chatter and I glanced over at Jace. His eyes darted around the room, nerves present on his face. I didn't necessarily like the kid, but I didn't want his brother hurting him either. Bryce was all talk, most of the time, but two-hundred bucks was probably enough to piss him off to the point of acting on it.

"Alright… Hey. Listen up." I spoke with authority from the back of the room. The laughter died down and eyes began darting in my direction. "We've been sitting here for days while Mr. Olsen drones on and on about the dangers of addiction and the effects of drugs on the human body and mind. Well, I'm a huge believer in show-don't-tell, so if you're wondering what the real effects of drugs are, you know where to find them." I nodded my head toward Jace. "This week only, there's a homecoming special." I sat back in my chair and watched as my classmates absorbed my words. Jace offered a fake smile to the students before directing his everything bagel/ doublemint breath back to me in an angry whisper.

"Homecoming special? What's that supposed to mean? I don't have anything special planned!"

"Offer a discount. You can afford it if you get enough customers."

"And if I don't get enough customers?" His already red face turned redder.

I looked back towards the class to see a thin-framed redhead with bright green doe eyes smiling seductively at me. She fluttered her eyelashes and pointed to her phone. I checked my messages, and sure enough. There was a message waiting for me.

RHONDA: Sign me up

I smiled back at her as she bit her lip and swayed slightly in her seat.

KIERAN: What do you want? And how much?

As I waited for Rhonda's response, I took a moment to survey the room. My sales pitch, albeit rushed and spontaneous, seemed to pique the interest of a few students throughout the room because a few of them were nodding at me and passing notes back with their numbers written on them. I shook off the guilt that was threatening to surface from the quiet realization that I was inviting others to indulge in a vice that I'd only barely escaped the grips of.

I slid the crumpled and ripped pages to Jace before I could think any better. "How'd you do that?"

"You just tell them what they want. And you let them know you have it." I leaned back in my chair again and returned my attention to my unread texts.

RHONDA: Which order will get me a night with you?

I raised my eyebrows in surprise. It's been a while since someone was so forward with me. I knew my reputation as the 'we can look but don't touch' guy. Not that I wasn't attracted to people at this school, I've just been secretly off the market for a while. But they wouldn't know that. They weren't supposed to.

KIERAN: Sorry love, I'm not on the menu. But get something hard enough and you might dream about it.

I didn't need to look at Rhonda to sense her disappointment. That wasn't my responsibility. I was just about to put my phone away when another message popped up on the screen.

B: English hallway closet. Between classes.

It took every ounce of willpower I had not to run to that closet right now. I tightened my hands into fists on the table and forced myself to think of something else. Anything but the prospect of what might happen in that closet in just a few short minutes. I rolled my eyes at my own reaction. 'Pathetic' I thought. I hated how much this person could affect me. One text and I was already a submissive mess. The cool, collected front I showed the world—while not entirely an act—was a lot more fragile than I let on. I knew myself and knew my desires too well. In everyday life, I liked to be in control, to dominate the conversations and the situations. But in my personal life, I was subservient through and through.

KIERAN: I'll be there.

Jace was buried deep in his phone like the pseudo businessman he was cosplaying as, a small smile creeping on his face. I could tell he had reached his quota. Good for him.

Time seemed to move impossibly slow and I tried to find something else to focus on, so that I wouldn't focus on the clock hanging above the door, taunting me with its miniscule movements. Apart from Callum, who spoke energetically with the son from his host family, Max, and Rhonda who had struck up a conversation with Emma and Ashley, the other cheerleaders in the class, the room was quiet.

But no one was as quiet as Dawn Price.

She was completely shrouded in a black hoodie that hung at least three sizes too large for her frame. Not that I knew much about her frame, she always wore clothes that concealed more than they revealed, as if she was trying to hide in plain sight. I'd only spoken to Dawn once before, on some random Thursday during the summer. She'd reached out to Jace, asking to buy some pills. Jace was on vacation, so I stepped in and met her under the bleachers just before nightfall.

"Dawn, right?" I remembered being surprised when I saw her approach. She didn't look like the normal customer Jace usually got. I remembered her eyes mostly, they were empty, haunted. Reminded me a lot of myself honestly.

"Yeah...um... How does this work?" Her voice was timid and fragile. Definitely a first-timer.

"Well, you already talked details with Jace right? You hand me the money and I hand you the bag."

She sniffled quietly and looked to the ground before rummaging through her pockets.

"Right, here. Sorry." She handed the small wad of cash over and I smiled.

"First time, huh?"

"What?" Her face went red and her eyes widened in horror.

"First time buying?" I clarified, confused as to why my original statement received such a response.

"Oh.. yeah." She kept her eyes trained on the ground at her feet.

"Alright, so you might wanna start with half. Can be pretty intense the first time around."

She nodded quietly, her wide brown eyes glistening with the beginnings of tears. A better man would have asked her what was wrong. Actually, a better man wouldn't have sold her the drugs in the first place.

But I was not a better man.

I found out a few days later why Dawn was so tormented that night under the bleachers. The video circulated pretty quickly, but I wasn't the most 'in' with the gossip. As far as sex tapes go, it wasn't the most graphic I had seen. Dawn's face was the only visible one. Her partner's identity remained hidden, which quickly turned into a game. Betting pools were passed around, people started making their own reaction videos, discussing their take on who the 'Dawn Banger' could be. My name was even tossed out as a potential partner a few times. Frankly, I didn't care, but I knew things were a lot different for women. I felt bad for Dawn. I didn't even know her, but she didn't deserve that.

Unfortunately, my first thought when I saw the video was pretty selfish. *God, I'm going to be screwed if she uses those pills...* But the second thought hit me like a punch to the gut, a rush of pure concern for Dawn. It wasn't that long ago that I had hit rock bottom myself and somehow found a way to keep digging. So, I did what any sane person would do, I tracked down her address through Juan, the weird computer hacker kid at school, and drove by her house. I wasn't sure what I was planning to do, but I had to know she was okay. Had to know she wasn't hurt.

I parked across the street and sat, watching. A tightly wound, professionally dressed woman stepped out of a car with a younger kid. The kid bounced around, full of energy. 'Okay, that's a good sign,' I thought to myself. I scanned the house, eyes lingering on the windows. Most of them were covered in curtains and blinds, blocking any chance of peering inside. I watched as the woman and the kid disappeared into the house. Two hours I sat there, waiting for some sign of Dawn, anything that might ease my conscience.

Just as the night started to settle and the street lamps flickered on, I saw a small figure pull back a curtain on the second floor. My heart jumped. I sank lower in my seat, the seat belt digging into my waist as I leaned forward, straining for a better look. The tension I didn't even realize I was holding started to unravel when I saw Dawn.

I could make out the brokenness in her face, even from

this distance, but that wasn't what mattered right then. She was alive. I turned the car on and sped away, the weight in my chest lifting slightly.

But now, seeing her sitting in class with that same hollow expression, part of me wanted to understand, wanted to ask her what happened, to reach out. But what good would that do? I wasn't a savior... I was the one who needed saving.

You could help her, you know? Introduce her to me.

The voice whispered through my mind as I watched Dawn from across the classroom. He was a constant presence I had grown accustomed to... my Angel. At first, his words had been chilling, almost menacing, but now they were a source of comfort. His voice had become my refuge, a personal security blanket I could wrap myself in. It was like a symphony of safety, each whisper a reminder that I was never truly alone. So, I didn't mind when he spoke to me throughout the day, offering advice or revealing things I hadn't even known were possible.

You're safe with me.

Those were the first words I heard from him that night when I almost fell over the edge.

"Who are you?" I whispered through dry, cracked lips at the shadowed figure that loomed over me.

Your Savior.

"Why me?"

Because you are worth saving, Kieran Andras.

My guardian. My savior. My Angel.

He told me I was worth saving, and I believed him. That was all it took.

I remember the way his darkness embraced me, calm, endless, like a moonless sky. It wasn't cold or terrifying. It was warm, protective, and for the first time in what felt like forever... I felt loved.

Over the past year of carrying this Angel in my mind, I came to realize something beautiful. He wasn't just mine. The closer I got to others, the closer he seemed to get to them too. When I opened up to someone, shared a part of myself, it wasn't just my heart that was exposed, it was his reach. Being intimate with someone, whether emotionally or physically, meant they too had the chance to be saved, if they needed it. And that thought filled me with a sense of purpose. I wasn't just being healed, I was sharing that healing, helping others find the peace that I had found. Maybe I had already helped someone. Maybe I was helping them right now.

Or maybe I'd never get the chance to.

My eyes trailed across the room to land on a frequent star of my thoughts.

Nani Ka'Ana was a new transfer from Hawaii. Their dad had just relocated for a job at the airport, and they only attended two weeks of junior year before summer vacation. Not nearly enough time to make any lasting connections before everyone scattered to their separate circles of friends for the summer. I first saw Nani at the skatepark, having swapped their surfboard for a skateboard. They were attempting some risky move that I was pretty sure was going to end badly if I didn't step in. I walked up, and the moment I saw their face, I knew. There was desperation, loneliness, anger, a hunger for something more. It was the same look I'd seen in the mirror every day before I met the Angel. I could feel the weight of it. That's why I approached them that day.

"Haven't you ever heard that you shouldn't stunt while angry?" I said, teasingly. I remember the day feeling warm, the sun was hidden behind a blanket of clouds, but its warmth still shone through. I remember being taken aback by how handsome Nani's bronzed face was. They had striking bone structure and deep-set brown eyes that seemed too troubled and too complex for anyone to attempt to comprehend. Their shoulder-length silky brown hair flowed casually in the slight breeze as I approached. They tossed their board down onto the grass at their feet and sat down on a bench near the bowl. I took a tentative step forward.

"You ok?" I prompted from my standing position behind them.

"Does it look like I'm alright?" Their voice had a gentle, melodic quality to it, a smooth rhythm that carried the warmth of their Hawaiian roots. The accent was unique, effortless, and almost musical in its flow. It wasn't something I could easily describe or imitate, but it was undeniably captivating. There was a natural beauty to it, like the soft sway of trees in the breeze.

"No. It doesn't. Mind if I sit?" I motioned toward the spot on the bench next to them and waited for a response. Nani glanced up at me, then shrugged, their gaze quickly returning to the bowl. They shifted over slightly, making room.

I lowered myself onto the bench, sitting sideways so I could face them directly. As I settled, I noticed Nani's build. They were muscular and toned, clearly an athlete. Their hands were rough and calloused, worn from hard work. It was clear they had spent more time doing physical labor than most kids our age, and it gave me a sense of the kind of life they had led, and sent a shockwave of recognition through me. Growing up too fast might be something we have in common.

"I'm Kieran. Kieran Andras."

They took a deep breath before turning to look at me. As our eyes met, I noticed them relax. "Nani Ka'Ana."

"Hello Nani." I couldn't help but smile at them. There was no denying that the person sitting in front of me was incredibly attractive, but it was the brokenness beneath that caught my attention the most. Something about their fractured pieces felt achingly familiar, like an echo of something I recognized within myself, whether I wanted to or not. "You're new here, right?"

"What gave it away? The accent, or the fact that you've never seen me before?" Nani snapped, their words laced with venom. I lowered my gaze, noticing how their strong, weathered hands gripped the edge of the bench with an ironclad hold, veins bulging along their forearms. Anger issues were, regrettably, another one of the traits I found myself drawn to in a partner. Textbook childhood trauma response.

"I've seen what it looks like when people get broken by this town," I said, my voice steady but tinged with understanding. "So, no. You've got something else going on, don't you?"

Nani took a silent moment to survey me, their eyes scanning me with a piercing intensity. My heart rate quickened at the thought of their gaze lingering on me like that, almost as if they could see something I didn't want them to. I quickly pushed the thought down, focusing on the words hanging between us instead.

"That's a pretty Kākā pickup line, Mō'ī'o. Does telling someone they're broken usually work for you?"

I couldn't contain the laugh of surprise that erupted from my throat. Nani cracked a small smile before turning their head to the bowl again.

"Once or twice. But tell me... was I wrong?" I inched closer on the bench and I could see the wave of tension course up through Nani's body as they sat straighter.

"No. You weren't wrong." Nani turned their head back to me and their eyes searched my face.

"So.. tell me. Who is Nani Ka'ana?" I asked, leaning my arms back to rest on the open bench behind me.

"Not much to tell. Lost my mom young to cancer. Lived most of my life in Honolulu. Spent my days at school and my nights surfing. Got moved here by my dad when he got a new job. And now I'm a Cactus Shadows Falcon, the end."

There was a pregnant pause before I responded.

"I'm sorry. About your mom. About leaving your home."

Nani narrowed their eyes on me.

"So, what's your story, 'Ono?" Nani's body relaxed as they spoke.

"It's not a fun one."

"Are they ever?"

"Touché" I laughed. I took a quick breath to gather my strength before continuing. "Born to junkie teen parents who loved drugs more than they loved having a kid. By seven, I was on a first-name basis with the paramedics who came when they overdosed. At fifteen I applied for emancipation and won. Went on an extreme drug bender. Not sure there's a single one I didn't try. But then... someone told me I was worth saving, so I got sober." I pulled the ten month sober chip out of my pocket and showed them. "And that's me."

"Well, E lālā."

I glanced at them questioningly.

"Shit," they clarified.

We both let out tense and breathy laughs before calmly letting silence take over.

"Can you keep a secret?" I inched closer again, lowering my head so that I was almost whispering in Nani's ear. Nani's body responded to the proximity, goosebumps covered their arms and they leaned into my whisper.

"Absolutely," Nani angled their head until they were mere inches away from my face. I could feel their cool breath tickle my nose.

"I'm broken too." I smiled and slowly licked my bottom lip before taking it between my teeth. Nani's eyes darted to my mouth and they let out a small sigh before smiling back. My entire body tingled, my own pleasure straining against the tight material of my jeans. It had been a while since a stranger had this kind of effect on me. I wanted nothing more than to grab Nani's face in my hands, and disappear into each other, ignoring the entire world around us. And from the look that Nani was returning, I thought that they might be feeling the same.

Help them, Kieran. You know what to do.

"Maybe we can be broken together, 'Ono." Nani's bold statement was all I needed to hear before reaching for their face and closing the space between us. I pulled my body as close to Nani's as the bench would allow and kissed them. They eagerly responded, opening their mouth to let my tongue dance with theirs. I gripped a handful of Nani's long hair tightly in my hand and they moaned into the kiss, which only ignited my fire even more. My free hand snaked around Nani's waist and pulled them into me, my eager body aching to be near them. Breaking free from the kiss, I trailed kisses down Nani's chin, onto their neck, pausing for just a moment to savor the delicious sounds they made.

Through breathy moans, they asked, "Do you... Greet every new kid like this?"

Lost in desire, I lifted his head to meet Nani's eyes again, the burning passion in their eyes undoubtedly mirrored my own. Nani's own arousal was evident from the way their chest heaved and their pupils dilated.

"Only the ones that look like you."

Nani closed the gap again and hungrily kissed me. The world slipped away, and the park faded from view as we stumbled, entangled, into the park's concrete restroom. Without breaking the kiss we spilled through the door. Once inside, I pulled back momentarily to flip the lock on the door. Locking the outside world out. Nani's wild eyes watched me as I slowly removed my black leather jacket and let it fall to the floor. Nani reached for the hem of their shirt and pulled it over their head, revealing their toned and tanned torso. My eyes feasted on their form, watching with fire burning in my core. My entire body tingled with the promise of pleasure.

"You look... delicious," I whispered before reaching for my own shirt slowly, teasingly, my eyes locked on Nani.

"You're taking too long." Nani rushed over and practically ripped my shirt over my head. They trailed kisses down my chest, and across the planes of my stomach as their hands worked meticulously with the button of my jeans. My breath caught in my throat as Nani lowered themselves to their knees in front of me, their eyes angled up at me, framed under dark lashes. I was nearly undone at that moment.

"Hmm, you look even better from down there," I whispered.

A vicious smile spread across Nani's face as their fingers reached for my waistband, and slowly slid my boxers down my muscular legs until they sat pooled around my ankles acting as a makeshift restraint, holding me to this moment. As if I ever would want to leave. Nani's eyes scanned my exposed length, now freed from its cloth prison and aching for a piece of the handsome creature kneeling in front of me.

Nani didn't speak, but instead let their fingers trail up the sides of my legs, traveling achingly slow from my ankles to my calves, then to my knees. My entire body erupted in goose-bumps and Nani's expert hands traveled my legs toward the center of my desire. Their slender fingers slid closer and closer to where I needed them.

"Now who's taking too long?" I jested, but my voice was strained, breathy.

"Stand still, and be good, or I may have to punish you," Nani commanded, their tone devious and certain, confident and dominant. A deep moan echoed from my chest and I bit my bottom lip to keep from begging. Gone was the powerful man I had crafted for the world to see, and in his place was the perfectly content submissive, burning for the opportunity to give into Nani's every whim.

"Keiki maika'i." Nani said. I didn't know the meaning behind the words, but the praise was evident in their tone and it sent shivers down my spine. Nani leaned closer to my anxious length, their fingers traveling up the front of my thighs, setting my entire body on fire. The wave of ecstasy that ran through me was so powerful that I couldn't control my hands that went to Nani's hair, gripping tightly and beckoning them closer to my need. Suddenly Nani's hands were gone and I couldn't stop the whine from escaping.

"Now now now. If you don't keep your hands to yourself... I'm going to have to tie them up." Their hands slowly removed my eager palms from their hair and kissed each finger before letting my hands fall back to my side.

"Is that a promise?" I asked, my need echoed in my tone. Nani smiled as they rose slowly from their knees, gripping my white t-shirt in their hands. I watched them eagerly as they forcefully grabbed my wrists and bound them in the white material. I couldn't contain the shallow breaths as they left my lips. Once Nani was satisfied with their makeshift restraints, they grabbed the center of the t-shirt which now bound my wrists and thrust it up above my head until they slammed against the wall behind me. I moaned and Nani's lips neared my ear, their cool breath made me shudder.

"If you move your hands, I stop. Do you understand?" Nani asked, fully in control and they knew it.

"Oh fuck, Nani." I exhaled, my untouched length aching at the command.

"I said..." Nani's tongue licked up the side of my neck and

their left hand reached for a spot on my thigh, gliding closer and closer, until their deliberate fingers brushed my erection briefly before inching away again. "Do you understand, 'Ono?"

"I understand." It was no more than a whisper. A whisper of a submissive. Nani smiled and with one last push against the t-shirt, forcing my hands to the wall above me, they sunk back down onto their knees before me.

Nani's hands found my thighs again and I could barely contain my whimpers of need. Nani was taunting me, forcing me to wait. And fuck, I loved every torturous second.

"You have quite the body, Kieran. I'm impressed." Nani spoke inches from my erection, so close that I could feel their breath on the tip. My blood ran cold.

"Please." My head rolled back till it rested on the wall behind me. My hands gripped the t-shirt as I fought the urge to once again tangle my fingers in Nani's long brown hair.

"Are you begging, Mr. Andras?" Nani's fingers traveled to the inside of my thighs, the tender flesh and my breath caught.

"Yes. Fuck yes. Please." I bucked my hips forward, until my tip was millimeters from Nani's taunting mouth.

"Tell me what you want, 'Ono," Nani whispered, their mouth so close to making contact that I could feel the movement of air as they spoke, my length jerked in excitement. Their fingers moved closer to my center, lightly grazing my skin and sending a shockwave of pleasure through my body.

"Take me." I spat, diverting all my mental energy to my hands. Willing them to stay on the wall despite the ever-growing desire to grab at Nani.

"Say the magic word, Kieran." Nani's fingers gripped me and their lips moved against the tightened skin of my shaft.

"Please." I felt the electricity in my veins as Nani's warm tongue slowly and lightly traveled along my heated skin.

Teasing me. Their fingers were playing expertly with my most sensitive part.

"I can't hear you." Nani whispered against the tip of my length, their mouth opening slightly to allow their tongue to dance quickly against the flesh there, but it wasn't enough.

"Fuck, please Nani! Please! I need you." I screamed through gritted teeth. And Nani listened. Their lips parted and welcomed all of me into the warmth of their open mouth. I saw stars as Nani's lips hugged me tightly, their tongue eagerly tasting every inch that I had to offer. It was slow at first, Nani was taking their time getting used to my length. I could feel the back of their throat open to accept me and had to force myself to calm down, or I would end this perfect moment far too quickly. Nani's mouth tightened around me and I felt their teeth lightly graze my flesh. It was more than I could handle and my hands had moved before I could even realize. My fingers tangled in their hair and pushed them deeper onto me, feeling resistance as my length hit the back of their throat. And then it was gone. All of my pleasure, the hands touching my skin, the teeth grazing my sensitive length, all of it. Gone. I groaned in aggravation.

"I told you not to move your hands." Nani's voice was deep and vicious. Hungry.

I threw my hands back up above me until they were back in their rightful spot against the wall.

"I'm sorry," I whispered.

"You broke the rules. I should leave right now, leave you unfinished, unsatisfied." They threatened.

"No." I argued. My naked body itching for the feel of Nani's mouth on me again.

"Give me one good reason I shouldn't punish you?" I was achingly aware of how close Nani was to me, but they remained at a distance, not touching me.

"Punish me, Nani. But I need you. Now." Nani's lips curved wickedly and their hands reached for my length again. Sliding back and forth along my shaft with their rough hands before taking the head into their mouth.

"Nani, more, please. I can't take this teasing." My voice was the voice of a broken man. But I wasn't ashamed, hadn't I already admitted to them that I was broken?

It was Nani's turn to take the commands. They took me entirely into their mouth again, the head hitting the back of their throat roughly, expelling delicious sounds echoing from deep within them, sounds so alluring that I tried to memorize them. Nani feasted on me with reckless abandon, their tongue lapping up every inch of me as if I were a delicacy. My body tightened as I felt the warmth build up inside of me and I knew I wouldn't last much longer.

"God Nani, I'm close. I'm so close." I exclaimed, I felt the skin on my hands turn raw as I rubbed them against the concrete wall, forcing them to remain in their spot, not wanting to risk Nani leaving me when I was this close to falling over the edge.

Nani's answer came in the form of teeth grazing my skin and hands squeezing just below. Their mouth slid quickly up and down my shaft pushing me ever closer to completion.

"Yes! Oh... fuck." I cried out as I came, my body exploding in a wave of passion I hadn't felt in some time. My body tensed as I toppled over the ledge of pleasure. Nani wasn't finished with me though. They proceeded to savor me until my body stilled. I wanted to revolt as Nani's lips slid off of me, leaving me utterly and totally depleted. My muscles strained to keep me upright.

"My turn," Nani smiled, wiping their mouth and rising from their knees. My desire rose up within my stomach again as I slowly removed the t-shirt binding, my satisfied length twitching again at the promise of pleasuring them. I slowly moved until Nani was the one with their back against the wall and sunk down to my position, looking up at Nani through burning eyes. Nani practically ripped off their own pants until they stood naked in front of me, their own need glaringly obvious. I eyed them with a hungry gaze.

"Make me feel something again, Kieran." Nani's plea surprised me and had I not been in my submissive state, I might have asked what they had meant by it, asked why they needed to feel something, and how long had it been since they had. But it was not my turn to ask questions or give commands. And at that moment, with Nani's sculpted body in front of me for the taking, I listened. For this was a command I was happy to submit to.

***

THIRTY MINUTES LATER, a knock on the bathroom door shook Nani and me from our post encounter bliss. We chuckled while quietly donning our clothes before exiting the bathroom structure. Our flushed faces grew warmer under the suspicious and prying eyes of the man who was waiting outside. We slid by, hiding our laughter until we reached the bench where we first met just under an hour ago. Nani stopped short of the bench and collapsed dramatically into the grass, still attempting to catch their breath and I took a seat on the bench above them.

"Well that was…" I began.

"Unexpected." Nani finished, angling their head so their bright brown eyes could look at me. I searched their face, they were flushed, but the same desperation and loneliness I saw earlier still seemed present. My smile faded slightly. Maybe I hadn't made them feel anything.

"Unexpectedly good?" I prompted. Nani paused, directing their eyes up to the cloud filled sky and took a deep breath.

"Well, let's just say that I needed that distraction." Nani answered, not tearing their eyes from the expanse above them.

"I'm glad I could help." Laughing through the words, I joined Nani in looking upwards.

"With a body like yours, 'Ono, you can distract me anytime you want."

I didn't look at them, but smiled up at the sky. I had to agree, Nani's physique was impressive. Surfing definitely did their body good.

"What does that mean? 'Ono?" I loved the way it sounded coming off their tongue no matter what it meant.

"You'll Google it later," they responded with a coy smirk. "You always so submissive or was that just for my benefit?" They asked.

I raised an eyebrow in response. "I have to make the decisions and be in charge in so many aspects of my life, it's nice to let the control go every once in a while."

Nani nodded, then whispered, "See, I feel so out of control all the time, it's nice to be able to take it sometimes."

Together, we sat in comfortable silence, a quiet understanding passing between us. It was strange, this connection, how despite not knowing each other, it felt like we were perfect puzzle pieces falling into place. Maybe you didn't need to know a person completely to understand them, maybe all you needed was to feel their soul. And in that moment, I felt like I understood Nani in a way I couldn't quite explain. I felt... content. Happy.

For a brief second, my mind wandered, imagining what it would be like to commit to someone, to build something real. I should have known not to dream.

I can't help them.

"Why not?" I blurted, forgetting where I was.

"Why not, what?"

"Um.. why not distract each other more often?" I composed myself and hoped it was enough to convince Nani.

"I'd certainly be interested in that."

I heard the hunger in their voice beckoning for me to respond, but chose not to meet their eyes. Instead, I looked inward, hoping for my Angel to explain.

I help lost souls, Kieran.

'I know that' I replied in my mind. 'Why can't you help them?'

Because Nani's soul isn't lost. It's gone.

'What?! How is that possible?' The silence between Nani and I became tense. I wasn't sure if Nani could feel it too. But I knew it was time to go, and quickly.

"Well, Nani Ka'Ana, I hope this isn't the last time we meet. I should go." I did my best to mask the confusion and worry in my voice.

"So soon?"

I must have done a good job at disguising my shock because Nani had flipped onto their stomach in the grass and was slowly checking me out with their empty brown eyes.

"I've always been a fan of round two."

I felt myself tighten with need but forced a calming breath.

"Round two will have to wait. Take care of yourself. No more angry stunts, alright? You'll get yourself killed." Nani's face fell and their bronzed complexion seemed to pale as they sat up in the grass.

"Yeah." And that seemed to be it. I narrowed my eyes at Nani's reaction, but decided it was better to leave it be. I stood from the bench and turned to make my way back to the junk storm, my loving nickname for my piece of crap car, that was waiting in the parking lot when I heard Nani call after me. "Hey... Thanks."

I turned and offered a soft smile before retreating to my car.

A lot of things you never thought were possible, are. There's so much more to this world than you could ever imagine.

And that was the last time my Angel spoke about it. And it was the last time Nani and I spoke, too.

A little over two months passed, and Nani seemed to have found a place among the others. I'd catch glimpses of them with Dawn, the two of them laughing and chatting like old friends. Well Nani would laugh, I can't remember the last time I saw Dawn smile. Nani would sit with her at lunch, and they'd often walk the halls together, side by side. At first, I felt a small, irrational twinge of jealousy, but I quickly shut it down. I had no right to feel that way. I had no claim on this handsome, ruggedly beautiful person. This... soulless creature.

Then one day, Nani walked into homeroom, and I couldn't help but smile at the sight of them. A fleeting smile, spawned from a moment of passion that was still fresh in my memory. Nani gave a polite, brief smile in return but quickly lowered their gaze and took a seat near Dawn. That was it. A few smiles exchanged in passing, nothing more. It felt like our shared moment had become nothing more than a whisper of history, fading into the background of everything else.

Every so often, I'd catch myself watching Nani smile and chat with Dawn, or catch them reading in the hall, or sitting in class with the back end of their pen casually between their lips. A "distraction," they had once called it. And what a distraction it was. Because by the time I'd imagined what it would feel like to be that pen, held in their hands, gently rolling between their lips, the bell rang, pulling me back into the present, signaling the start of the fleeting six-minute break between classes.

I sprinted out of the room, slamming into a towering figure.

"Watch where you're going!" they snapped, their voice echoing through the halls as I kept moving, unbothered by the accidental run-in. I could feel Nyx's eyes searing into my back, radiating a fury I wasn't in the mood to test. But right now, that didn't matter. There was something, or rather, someone, waiting for me, and nothing was going to slow me down.

CHAPTER 2

BACK IN THE FUCKING CLOSET

DODGING THROUGH CLUSTERS OF STUDENTS, I reached the closet within a minute, heart pounding. Tucked away in a small alcove, the area housed a couple of storage rooms, the janitor's closet, and the school's makeshift suspension room. I stepped up to the supply closet- the door already cracked open. A few weeks ago, my rendezvous partner had snagged a key, transforming this into our secret midday escape. Slipping inside, I pulled the door shut behind me, letting the darkness swallow us whole.

"You made it," Brett Jacobs whispered in a low commanding tone. Goosebumps erupted across my skin, my length already straining against my jeans. I couldn't see him, but I could feel his presence. God, how I loved his presence. Before I could respond to him, Brett pinned me up against the closed door and kissed me feverishly, with no holds barred, no tenderness, no love. Just pure, unbridled, and self-loathing passion. His lips devoured mine, his tongue demanding entrance. "We've got four minutes. Make it worth it," Brett whispered in my ear and I quickly removed my clothes and joined Brett in the feral frenzy. This wasn't like it was with Nani, no, I hadn't felt comfortable enough to hand over the reins entirely to Brett like I did with Nani all those months ago. With Brett it was like two people each with a hand on the driver's wheel, not working together, but fighting for control. And it was like a drug in its own right to me. The fight, the anger, the relentless hatred. It mixed together to create the perfect self-loathing cocktail. And it was irresistible.

These moments of passion were not drawn out, not lavished. They were quick, satisfying, and mind-numbing. Exactly what I needed.

I admired Brett's physique, and in the darkness of the closet I allowed myself to feel every inch of him. My hands were exploring Brett eagerly as he turned around facing away from him. Brett spoke over his shoulder at me.

"Now, Andras. Fuck me. We're wasting time."

I smiled devilishly at Brett, preparing myself to take him.

"Now. Make it quick." Brett commanded again and I wasted no time before entering Brett with a forceful thrust.

"Fuck..." Brett's voice caught in his throat and he moaned as I made quick work of his pleasure, bringing myself to the edge of my own release. "More Kieran. Please."

I sped up, my hands digging into Brett's hips and I drove into him. I reached forward and gripped Brett's length tightly and squeezed as I began stroking him. "Kieran. Yes. Kieran."

"Come for me," I ordered through gritted teeth and Brett obeyed, which sent me tumbling after him in ecstasy. My body curled around his as I let pleasure wash over me. My heart pounded against my chest, beating in my ears and I took deep breaths. These were the moments I loved the most. These quiet moments with Brett when our pleasure was all-consuming, when we were so spent, so deeply connected that words didn't matter. I wished these moments could last longer.

Because I hated what came after them. Brett moved quickly, sliding himself off of me before replacing his pants.

I hastily fastened the buttons of my jeans as the loud sounds from the hallway died down. The bell would ring shortly.

"You know it'd be easier to get dressed if the lights were on." I laughed.

"Someone might see the light under the door." Brett answered brashly, a stark contrast from the man who was just moaning my name.

"I had fun," I prompted, hoping for some kind of acknowledgement from Brett that he, too, enjoyed himself.

"If anyone asks, you never saw me."

I couldn't help but roll my eyes. Our little 'arrangement' had been secret for over four months now.

We were partnered up for an English project at the end of last year. Together, we had to read and lead a presentation on the book of our choice. We met in the computer lab after his team's workout one night. The school was nearly empty save for a few teachers and the students permitted to use the labs. We were the only ones in the classroom that night. I sometimes wonder what might have happened differently had we not been.

"I don't care what we pick. I probably won't read it. So, if you want me to do any work, pick something that's on sparknotes." Brett Jacobs annoyed me to no end. His cocky attitude, the way he sat back in every chair and put his feet up on whatever was in front of him- it was all enough to make me want to rip his head off. He had dark brown skin and short black hair. He was lean and muscular, a testament to his athleticism. I might have considered him hot, if I didn't hate him so much.

"Thanks for being honest." I said, rolling my eyes. "Ready

Player One. It's got a lot of pop culture references. You might not hate it."

"Whatever." Brett sat with his phone in his hands, his thumbs furiously typing away on the keyboard. I watched him, thinking about what a shame it was that someone so hot was an absolute asshat.

"Jesus Christ, Brett. Will you put your phone down for one goddamn minute and talk about this project with me? Unlike you, I don't have a football scholarship waiting for me after school. I need to get out of here on my own."

Brett paused and slowly slid his phone into his pocket.

"Why do you even care? Not like your parents will get mad that you missed an assignment," Brett said casually, as if he wasn't throwing the most terrible fact of my life in my face. I snapped. In a flash, my hands were around Brett's throat and I had him tipped back in his chair so far that if I were to let go, Brett would topple to the ground.

"Dude, what the hell!?" Brett thrashed carefully against my hold, his eyes darting to the ground behind him.

"Anyone ever tell you that you're an asshole?" I whispered into Brett's ear before slowly returning him to an upright position and dropping my hands from his throat. Brett only waited a moment before he was out of his seat and pushing me up against the wall. His right forearm pressed firmly across my neck while his other hand was steady against the wall just next to my head, caging me in.

"What did you call me?" Brett's fury was palpable, I remember feeling the burning in his eyes as he scanned my face.

"Fuck you." I forced as much venom as I could into my voice. I wanted it to hurt. At the time, Brett's face looked like one of anger, of pure murderous intentions. I would have bet a lot of money that Brett was going to hit me right there.

Never in a million years would I have guessed that he would lean forward, his arm still firmly pressed onto my throat, and kiss me. Brett's mouth angrily covered mine, his tongue ripping through the barrier of my lips until it reached mine.

"What the hell are you doing?" I yelled, pushing a flustered Brett back, but not exiting the intimate space between us.

"Don't tell anybody." Brett pleaded. At that moment, I had a few choices. Out him to everyone, which would be shitty, but hey Brett's a shitty person so why should I care? Walk the fuck away and forget this whole thing happened. Or enjoy this moment of forbidden pleasure with the handsome asshole who kisses like his life depends on it. I watched Brett's eyes. They were scanning my face, asking for permission to continue.

He needs my help. So, help yourself.

With that word of encouragement from my Angel, I reached up, grabbed Brett's face and kissed him, a mixture of passion and fury, teeth and tongues until we were ripping at each other's clothes, letterman and leather jackets being tossed to the ground. Jocks may be inept and cruel, but they sure are ripped. I remember the first time I explored the plane of Brett's stomach. His perfectly sculpted body was so fascinating that I couldn't stop myself from tracing the outlines of his ab muscles with my fingers, then my tongue. That was the first time Brett called out my name, but it was most definitely not the last.

Throughout the summer, Brett would pay me visits at my studio apartment. I lived on the so-called 'bad' side of town, so Brett never had to worry about being spotted. And with no roommates, it was an easy enough arrangement. The summer was spent in a glorious bubble of passion. No rushed closet quickies, no worrying about the lights on... just us. We never defined the relationship. Never said we had to be exclusive. In fact, Brett often spent his evenings after he left me with his girlfriend Ashley. I would have felt bad for her if Ashley wasn't a downright bitch. When school started, things changed. I was working so much that time at my studio was limited, and Brett was in season for football. So, this little closet arrangement was born out of necessity, need, and desire for each other. But it brought out a side of Brett that I hated. The side that was closeted and afraid, the side that punished me for being able to be myself unapologetically while Brett couldn't. Not that I didn't like a little punishment every once in a while, but only when it was consensual.

"I'm getting pretty tired of this," I said quietly, but with enough force that Brett had stopped getting dressed and paused in the dark closet.

"What?" Brett's anger was thinly veiled.

"This. You somehow got me to literally go back into the closet. Every time we're here you act like I'm the best sex you've ever had, then treat me like a mistake the next second. Yet, I keep coming back."

"You keep coming back because it *is* the best sex I've ever had. And I can bet the same for you." For a brief, anger filled moment, I wanted to tell him he was wrong. To tell Brett about the encounter with Nani that replayed in my mind almost nightly as I pleasured myself to the memory of their lips on my body. Nani and I never even had sex, but it was still the best experience I'd ever had, but I didn't wanna share that moment with anyone. Not in spite, or for revenge. It was just for me. So instead I just sighed.

"I'm not ok with being a secret anymore, Brett. I want to go public with us." I reached across the empty space until I found Brett's hand and squeezed.

"You know I can't do that." The anger in Brett's voice was replaced with fear.

"You can. I'll help you. You care about me, don't you?" My hands gently grazed Brett's forearms, caressing them.

"You can't do that to me. You can't guilt me into coming out. That's not fair. Besides, I'm not gay." Brett pulled back and continued dressing. I had lost count of how many times I've heard that phrase come out of Brett's beautiful, stupid mouth. 'I'm not gay' he'd say as my hands ran along his body. 'I'm not gay' he said between kisses, literally forced to pull his tongue from my mouth to even say the words. 'I'm not gay' he'd say as I thrust into him from behind. I ignored it most of the time. Once I even tried to help, it didn't go well. Brett was over my house, we had just indulged in each other, and I thought it was a good time to bring it up.

"Ok. Let's say you're not. Maybe you're bi then? Or pan like me. Gay is not the only term out there, ya know." It was mid June, warm and stifling.

Brett removed himself from my bed and angrily donned his shirt.

"You're trying to force me to be something I'm not, Kieran," he said.

"No, I'm trying to help you find out what you are," I retorted before crawling across the bed on my hands and knees towards where Brett stood. I remember placing my hands on Bretts arms and pulling him back so that he stood just at the edge of the bed.

"I'm not like you, you know." Brett spat, his anger mixing with passion as my hands continued to roam his body,

"Ok." I said softly as I lifted the bottom hem of Brett's shirt and revealed his lower abdomen and planted slow sensual kisses along his hip muscles. I watched Brett's desire grow beneath the fabric of his boxers.

"This is purely physical." Brett said. I had heard that before too and I agreed at the time.

"Whatever you say." I spoke against Brett's skin, my cold breath leaving goosebumps on Brett's dark skin causing him to curse under his breath.

"Fuck, Kieran." And Brett was undone. The argument would surely come again another time, but I, in my perfect summer bubble of sexual bliss, refused to let it get to me. I would bask in the afterglow of forbidden love for as long as I could take it. A part of me knew that I would eventually hit a breaking point. But back then it seemed so far away.

Apparently, it wasn't that far at all, because today I felt myself soar past the breaking point as Brett muttered those fucking words again.

Anger rushed through me in that moment and as if some unknown force was pushing me to speak my mind, I said, "You were pretty fucking gay two minutes ago, Brett. And on Monday. And last Thursday and, oh right, just about three times a week for this entire school year! And don't even get me started on this summer." It felt so good to unload like that, a different kind of rush, that I just kept going.

"Be quiet, Kieran," he urged, his eyes anxiously glancing toward the door as my voice soared.

"Listen, you're a good lay, but I've had better and truthfully, I don't deserve to be someone's dirty little secret. And I'm not gonna be with someone who's ashamed to be with me." I turned on my heel and threw open the closet door illuminating the small space and Brett's face for the first time. His dark brown skin was smooth and inviting, his face stoic and unchanging, but I noticed a small trail of tears falling from his perfect brown eyes. I spent so long avoiding eye contact with him in the halls that I had forgotten just how gorgeous he was.

It took everything I had in that moment to pull myself back from falling into his eyes again.

"What are you saying, Kieran?" Brett whispered just loud enough for me to hear.

"I'm saying goodbye, Brett." I stepped out of the closet and into the hallway, refusing to glance back. The sound of the bell echoed through the corridors, signaling the start of a new class and the end of us. With steady steps, I moved forward, leaving Brett and everything we'd been behind me.

CHAPTER 3

TRUST ME, I'M AN ADDICT

It took all my willpower to resist texting Brett as the rest of the week crawled by. Thankfully, we didn't share any classes. I wasn't sure how I'd handle the weight of his deep brown eyes boring into the back of my head during a lecture. Would I regret walking away? I shook the thought off, refusing to let it take root.

"Get a fucking grip dude," I whispered to myself just as the bell rang for students to move on to their lunch period.

Lost in the tug-of-war between my mind and my body, I failed to notice the crowd until I collided with someone who had stopped to watch. They turned around sharply, their eyes narrowing before they let out an exaggerated sigh and rolled their eyes at me.

"Are you doing this on purpose or something?" Nyx Channery spoke, their voice was a deep timbre, not quite animalistic, but it had a harshness to it that made me believe there was a whole lot of anger pent up in that one person.

"No. Sorry." I didn't want to get into it. I was pretty sure that Nyx could kick my ass and I wasn't particularly in the mood to test that theory. "What's going on?"

Nyx rolled their eyes and turned back toward the crowd. "That Max kid is like freaking out or something. Looks like a seizure." Max? I thanked Nyx under my breath before weaving my way through the crowd. The closer I got, the more I heard. A few students were down on the ground with Max holding him steady while others had run off to get a teacher.

My breath hitched when I saw Max. His pale skin glistened with sweat, his lips tinted an unsettling shade of blue. Bloodshot eyes stared vacantly, and his body trembled, wracked by an invisible force. The sight was painfully familiar, etched into my memory so deeply that I moved forward instinctively, unable to stop myself.

"He's overdosing. Someone call 911 now!" I fell to the ground replacing one of the girls who was crying over Max's writhing body. I grabbed his head and held it in my hands. "Ok, Max. Stay with me. Hey you, what's your name?"

The small girl who's spot I took looked back and forth between Max and I. Clearly in a state of shock, she didn't answer. I recognized her face, she was in my grade, but I couldn't place her name. She kept to herself mostly. I heard she had a college boyfriend or something.

"Hey, listen to me!" I snapped, drawing her wide-eyed gaze from Max's form.

"Sorry... I'm Hannah." She answered nervously.

"Help me get him to his side," I barked.

She did. Her delicate fingers held Max's head steady as I shifted his body to the side.

"Who called 911?" I asked the question to no one in particular, my voice barely more than a whisper, my gaze locked on the boy in front of me. He looked so young, far too young to be caught in the grips of something so...violent. My heart clenched painfully as an unwelcome image flashed in my mind of my own body twisting and convulsing just like his.

The memory surged, vivid and haunting. I swallowed hard, forcing the image back into the shadows where it belonged. This wasn't about me. Not now.

But as I looked at Max, trembling and fighting against forces too great for him to control, I couldn't escape the reflection of myself that I saw in him. His pain mirrored mine, his fear felt like my own.

I shook my head, focusing every ounce of my willpower on the present. Max needed me, needed someone to fight for him, to pull him back from the brink. Because I knew, better than anyone, what it felt like to gaze into that abyss and have no idea if I would ever escape it.

"I did!" Salem Bridges stepped forward out of the crowd. "They're on their way. They say to get him on his side."

"Yeah. And they're gonna say check for a pulse too." I did. "It's there. Weak, but it's there. Shit." Max's mouth foamed with a sickly, greenish ooze that bubbled and spilled over his lips, sliding down his chin in streaks.

"What the hell?" I whispered under my breath. I'd seen the effect of just about every drug overdose out there. This was not one I recognized. "What the fuck did you take, Max?"

"Yeah. He said he did already. Weak but there." Salem hurriedly spoke into the phone just as Mrs. Smith burst through the crowd.

"Everyone back to class now!" The crowd began to disperse as other teachers began herding the masses away. Salem stepped forward towards Mrs. Smith.

"911 is on their way," she told her. Mrs. Smith thanked her quickly and then hurried to my side.

"Mr. Andras, go to class, we can handle this." But the nervous twitch above her right eyebrow and the unsteadiness of her hands told me otherwise.

"With all due respect, Mrs. Smith, I'm willing to bet a lot of money I've seen more overdoses than you. I'm staying."

She didn't argue. Instead, she placed her hands on his head and relieved Hannah. "Hannah, I've got this. Thank you."

She did not have to be told twice. Her scared and small frame got up and almost sprinted down the hall. At least she stepped forward at all, I thought. That was more than any of those other kids did.

I looked at Mrs. Smith who was taking deep breaths, and holding Max's head off the ground.

"As long as we can get some naloxone or something in him soon he'll have a good chance of recovery." I counted once, the longest that my parents had gone before receiving the life saving dose was one hour. Even I didn't know how long they could push it. And not knowing how long Max was down before I got there, I estimated they're about six minutes in now. I was too busy checking Max's pulse again to understand the overhead announcements, something about staying in the classrooms, no wandering... etcetera. The seconds moved in increments both blindingly fast and painstakingly slow. Each tick of the second hand on the hall clock was a taunting reminder that Max was lost somewhere in a liminal nothing-ness and we needed to hurry before he was gone forever. Eventually the paramedics arrived and I heard Salem graciously thanking the dispatcher.

"Yes, I see them, Thank you so much! They're here!" In a rush of movement, the paramedics were in and had replaced Mrs. Smith and I on the ground near Max.

"Down about ten minutes I'm guessing. Still has a pulse, but it's weakening." I explained as the paramedics took their spots and readied the dose of naloxone. Mrs. Smith urged Salem and me to head back to class, but I gave her my best 'you're kidding me, right?' look, and she conceded. For a moment I relaxed, Max had been given the dose and the paramedics said he was stable enough to move. I let my head fall back in relief, I didn't realize how nervous I was for this random kid in my homeroom class.

As my gaze wandered upward, something caught my attention, a flicker of movement where there shouldn't have been any. My breath hitched. A face was poking through the ceiling tiles. Not through an open gap, but right through the solid material, like the tiles were intangible. The face was feminine, its features blurry and indistinct, like an image on a fogged-up mirror. I blinked, trying to focus, but before I could fully process what I was seeing, it vanished.

I shook my head, trying to ground myself. Whatever it was, I didn't have time to think about it. Besides, given my current state of mind, who's to say it was even real?

"Kieran. I should have guessed you were the one who knew exactly what to do." Laura Hines, paramedic, said as her colleagues helped lift Max onto a gurney.

"Laura. It's been a long time." I smiled slightly at her. During the last three years that I lived with my parents she was one of the regulars.

"What'd he take?" She asked. This was a question that very frequently, I had an answer for. I knew exactly what my parents had taken every time. Sometimes, I was even proud of myself for knowing the strand, or the specific things it was cut or laced with. But this time... I had no idea.

"I don't know. I didn't recognize it. Had some kind of green ooze coming out of his mouth."

Laura scrunched her eyebrows.

"Green ooze?" She repeated incredulously.

"Listen, I don't get it either. But that's what it was." I shrugged.

"Alright. Well hey, it's nice to see you. Although, I'm glad our visits aren't as frequent anymore." Her blue eyes looked saddened and the small crows feet at the corners of her eyes looked deeper, more prominent than the last time I saw her.

The words I desperately needed to say hung on my tongue. Acidic and painful. I could walk away, ignoring the burning empathy in my chest that felt so unwarranted, or I could ask. I could simply ask...

"How many?" I whispered, my voice barely audible. I wasn't sure I even wanted the answer, but I needed it.

Mrs. Smith glanced between us, her brow furrowed with confusion. I didn't care if she overheard.

Laura hesitated, shifting uncomfortably. "You know I'm not supposed to tell you that." Her eyes fell to the floor, avoiding mine.

"Please?" The word tasted foreign on my tongue. I wasn't used to begging...at least not outside the bedroom or, in Brett's case, the closet. But here I was, raw and exposed, pleading for a truth that might break me.

Laura let out a long, weary sigh. "In the last year... six."

The air was knocked out of me, the number acting like a fucking fist to my gut. I sucked in a sharp breath through my nose, nodding despite the ache spreading in my chest.

"Two for her," Laura added softly, her voice laced with guilt. "Four for him."

Each word felt like a needle, pricking deep into my skin.

"Are they...?" I paused searching for a way to finish my question. 'Okay' wasn't the right word. They haven't been okay in a long time, I knew that. And Laura did too.

"Alive. Yes." Laura's voice was gentle, her tone full of sympathy. The look in her eyes mirrored the one she'd given me across the courtroom when she testified on my behalf during my emancipation.

She told the judge I was more of an adult than most adults

she knew. That I'd been forced to grow up too fast, robbed of the chance to be a kid. She said I deserved a life free from the suffocating clutches of drugs.

If only she knew how far I'd fallen since then. How hard I had to claw my way back up. She'd be disappointed.

"Good," I said, my voice measured, slipping into the calm, detached tone I'd perfected over the years. I had long mastered the art of pretending to be fine with the cards life had dealt me. This was just another hand to bluff. "I didn't know what they'd do when no one was around to make the call for them anymore."

Beside me, Mrs. Smith let out a quiet sigh, the sound heavy with realization. The final puzzle pieces had clicked into place for her. I was talking about my parents.

My parents, the drug addicts.

It wasn't a secret. Not around town, not at school, much to my endless disdain. And now, Laura has confirmed it. Six times in the past year. Six times, someone was called to my old house to save my parents from themselves. Six times, they nearly died from their own addiction.

And I wasn't there to call for help anymore. I wasn't there to save them. To protect them. To keep them alive.

I stayed in that house for so long, ignoring the crushing weight of their addiction, ignoring what was best for me. I stayed not out of love but out of fear. Fear that if I wasn't there to dial 911, no one would be.

"I guess I'm glad they've taken turns OD'ing, so the other one can call for help," I offered with a humorless chuckle.

Laura looked like she wanted to respond to that, but couldn't find the words. I'm not sure there ever would be the right words for this.

"You look good, kid," she praised warmly, giving me a maternal smile.

"Sobriety will do that," I teased, and she gave me a knowing look and nodded.

"Yeah, it will."

"We're good. Let's go," the other paramedic stated once Max was secured to the gurney.

The principal was helping direct the paramedics to wheel Max out of the building, and I could see him slowly returning to a normal shade, his breathing evened out. I let loose a sigh of relief. Laura turned back to me. "I gotta go. Let's hope we don't see each other again. Hey, if you ever find out what he took, give the hospital a call. It always helps to know what it was. Take care of yourself, Kieran."

I nodded as Laura and the other paramedics took Max down the hall and around the corner.

"Mr. Andras, Ms. Bridges. Thank you for your help. Go ahead and head to class. I will call your teachers to excuse your tardiness. Feel free to take a moment in the restroom." She nodded to my shirt which had been a victim of the mysterious green ooze. "Thank you both. I'm so sorry you had to do that, and I'm so proud that you did." She spoke honestly, a hint of admiration in her tone, and she was off.

"Shit. Now I have to change my shirt." I gripped the hem of my shirt to inspect the damage. The green ooze had left a nasty looking circular stain near the bottom.

"Can I watch?" Her big eyes were looking up at me through a veil of long lashes.

"Salem. You're looking as tempting as ever today." Just because I chose not to sleep around as much during my time with Brett, didn't mean I couldn't flirt. And oh man, does Salem Bridges know how to flirt. Her skin was silky and her blonde hair looked thick enough to grab a hold of. We've never gone there, not sure I ever would, but I'd be lying if I said I didn't enjoy imagining it. Especially when she was near me. Her presence was like a damn siren song, forcing sinful images and thoughts to the forefront of my mind.

"And you've been prudent for too long, Kieran."

I laughed and she smiled, moving her hand up my arm. For a moment, my senses were lost to her touch. Her gaze held mine prisoner as if her irises were a padlock of desire. Her thick lips pouted at me, and her body beckoned me forward. My willpower was fucking nonexistent in her presence. I was about to step forward and indulge in the desire Salem was offering me when I heard the Irish calvary coming down the hall in the form of Callum Farroway.

"Where is Maxy? I just heard! Is he ok? What did you do?" Callum burst forward and gripped me by the collar of my stained shirt, effectively breaking me from whatever spell Salem's gaze had just had me under.

"Callum, dear. Kieran kept Max alive until the paramedics got here. You should be thanking him, not choking him." Salem placed a hand on his shoulder.

Callum looked from Salem back to me and for the first time I got a really good look at the lucky charm himself. His eyes were a bright golden brown with flakes that almost seemed to refract the light. His skin was smooth and unblemished and his dark hair was tightly wound in short bouncy curls. Callum slowly backed away from me and let his hands fall to his side. I adjusted my collar and raised an eyebrow to Callum.

"My apologies. You see Maxy's me closest pal and I just heard he had to be wheeled outta here in a state. Got a wee nervous." Callum's accent made it hard for me to understand his rambling at that speed. But one thing was evident, he was really worried about Max.

"No big deal, do you know what he took?" I asked abruptly.

"What he took?"

"The drugs. What drug did he take?" I clarified.

"He only smokes a little marijuana occasionally." Callum responded defensively.

"Yeah, well, he took something else today." I was suddenly very aware of the ooze stain on my shirt. "Something a lot harder."

"What are you on about? He wouldn't do that."

"And you can guarantee that? You can say with one hundred percent certainty that Max did not take any drugs today?" I let a little venom into my retort. Friends and family who refused to see the truth right in front of them were a part of the problem. I would know, I was one of them for a long time.

"Well... no." Callum slumped, looking over to Salem. "But can you guarantee that he did?"

Yes, I wanted to say. I'd seen enough overdoses to know one. But for whatever reason, Callum wasn't ready to hear that, so I said, "He's going to the hospital now. He'll be ok."

"Callum dear, you need to relax. You seem tense." She had snaked her way around behind him and slid her hands over his shoulders and began massaging. Callum's golden eyes turned vivid and he smiled.

"Salem, pet, is this truly the best time to get me excited?" Callum turned and I had half a mind to run the other way. The hypnotizing tunnel vision of desire I had just moments ago, a distant memory.

"Kieran was just about to strip for me. Wanna join us?" She cooed. I laughed and rolled my eyes. Narrowing my eyes at her, I was almost ready to accost her for being so forward, when Callum turned towards me, a glint in his eye. He didn't seem to dislike the idea.

"I'll see you later Salem, Callum." I hurried down the hall, leaving behind a flirtatious Salem and a very amused Callum, both grinning at each other. Guess Max wasn't weighing on Callum's mind as much anymore.

I was reminded of my shirt again. Luckily, I had an extra one in my gym locker, so I made a beeline for the locker room. As I stepped inside, I heard the sound of a shower running. It was unusual, just after lunch, no one should be showering from gym class at this hour. I brushed it off and headed to my locker, grabbing the first shirt I could find that wasn't soaked in sweat. I pulled off my leather jacket and the ooze-stained shirt, ready to slip into the fresh one.

But just as I was about to pull it over my head, a low whistle from behind me froze me in place. I hadn't even noticed the shower had stopped. I turned around, and there stood Nani Ka'Ana, towel wrapped low around their waist, their golden-brown skin glistening with water. Droplets clung to their long, wet hair before racing down their muscular torso and dripping onto their abs, following the natural lines of their body. I couldn't help but watch, my gaze fixated on the path the water took—down, down, down.

"Take a picture. it'll last longer." Nani smiled and began wringing their hair.

"I prefer more three dimensional art." My voice was clear, low, and welcoming. I hadn't realized just how much the sight of Nani had sent my blood running. My length twitching behind my jeans.

"I remember." Nani smiled. The air hung heavy between them. Me, shirtless and Nani covered only in a towel in an empty locker room.

"I'm getting a little deja vu here. It's not the first time we were shirtless in a bathroom together." I finished pulling my shirt on, because I knew if I didn't do it now, I never would. And no matter how incredibly tempting Nani looked at this moment, I 'broke up' with Brett less than a week ago and it was not time to jump right into bed, or shower, with someone else.

"If it was really like last time your shirt would be coming off, not going back on," Nani said with a laugh and I couldn't help but laugh with them. They had that kind of effect on people. Their laugh was like a calming summer wind. It was a big difference to the cool dread of warning that Brett evoked.

"How have you been, Nani?" Clutching their towel around their waist, Nani sat down on one of the benches that were sprawled out across the locker room. If I was a less decent man, my eyes may have been drawn to Nani's muscular upper thigh as the towel's overlapped edges fell open, but I was much too mature and composed for that. Instead, I focused on Nani's face, locking my eyes with theirs, determined to ignore the temptation of the bare skin they were showing. The towel, barely clinging to their waist, left little to the imagination, a thin layer of fabric that could easily be removed. A fact that I was all too painfully aware of.

"Been better." Matter of fact. Direct. No edge of flirtation. I fought against the urge to pout.

"Yeah. Same. Although we're both doing better than Max right now." I replied back just as directly. Nani should not know how much they affect me.

"Max? What happened to Max?" Nani's eyes widened. Worry seeped onto their face.

A pang of jealousy coursed through me. Were they together? Did Nani and Max have something going on? Why did Nani care so much?

"Looked like an overdose. He's ok. On his way to the hospital now." At that, Nani rose to their feet quickly.

"An overdose?" Nani disappeared behind one of the bays

of lockers and I heard the disappointing sounds of clothes being donned. I remained in my spot.

"Yeah. I've seen enough to know one. Are you two... close?" I regretted it the moment it came out. What kind of jealous asshole asks that kind of question?

"Not really, but he means a lot to Casper and she's kind of my homegirl." Relief followed by confusion.

"Casper?"

"Dawn." Nani said as they reemerged from behind the lockers, fully clothed.

"Interesting nickname." I chuckled humorlessly as a terrifying thought jumped into my head. The sex tape. What if it was Nani?

I only saw it once and I had stopped watching pretty quickly before I reported it. I liked my adult videos taken with permission of those involved, so I didn't get a very good look at who the other person was. I don't remember seeing Nani's signature tanned skin though.

"Well, you can let her know he's okay. For now."

Nani nodded and moved towards the exit.

"Thanks Special K." And they slipped out into the hall before I could respond.

I smiled at the nickname and followed Nani's lead and headed to the hallway.

So many people need our help, and you're drawn to the one we can't? The deep voice filled my mind.

"Do all of my relationships have to be with people you can help?" I half joked in a whisper as I traveled down the hall to my class.

Yes.

Shock flooded my chest at that. I knew that my Angel wanted to help others like me, but I never thought that my

Angel would dictate who I could and couldn't be around. "But, um.."

You're upset?

"No, that's not it.. I just. What if I want to be with someone who doesn't need your help?" The silence in my head was deafening as I waited for a response from my savior.

Are you displeased with our arrangement, Kieran?

The voice spoke with a venom that I had never heard from my savior before and it took me aback. I paused in the hall and moved up against the wall. I placed my forehead on the cool brick. It was a solid few seconds before I had the composure to respond.

"No. of course not. I just.."

You were just questioning me.

A chill ran down my spine, and my muscles tensed involuntarily. It was a fear response, I realized, but it felt so out of place. I had never been afraid of him before.

"I'm sorry. I didn't mean to..." I was scrambling. My angel had never sounded like this before, never so disappointed in me. I hated it. I hated that I had made a mistake. And for the first time in a long while, I couldn't shake the question that seeped into my head.

What would happen to me if my savior decided I was no longer worth saving?

Kieran. Kieran. Kieran.

His low simmering anger echoed in my head. This was not good.

Have I not been extremely generous with you? Have I not given you purpose?

"You have," I whimpered.

I offer to help others. And yet, you think you have the right to decide who deserves it? You think your judgment is more valuable than mine?

"No, of course not. I'm so sorry. I didn't mean it." My heart raced and my body filled with a silent dread.

If you would like to spend time with your soulless creature, you must do something for me.

"Anything you need." I desperately pleaded, my head pressing harder against the wall as if the pressure might counteract the growing fear.

Every time you are with Nani Ka'Ana, you must bring me someone of my choosing. Someone who needs my help. And you will not refuse.

"Of course." It was barely a whisper, the sounds of a broken man. My Angel left. There was nothing left to say. And there, with my head leaning up against the wall and tears threatening to fall, for the first time in over a year, I felt completely alone.

CHAPTER 4

TELL ME SOMETHING I DON'T KNOW

SEVENTH PERIOD DRAGGED ON. The whole afternoon did. My body was fatigued, and I felt heavy, as if someone had replaced my organs with sandbags that weighed me down. I sunk into my chair. The angel had never spoken to me like that. Never commanded me that way. I was scared. My mind swirled with the consequences of this partnership. I hadn't questioned it for the entire year that my angel lay in wait in my mind. But now. What if this wasn't what was best for me. What if this wasn't an angel at all?

I was so lost in thought that I didn't register the ringing bell. The class emptied quickly and I sat in my chair, feeling too heavy to move. I took a deep breath and began to rise from my seat, slowly, unwillingly.

"Kieran." The voice called from behind me. It wasn't a voice I heard often, but it was one I knew. I turned slowly to face Dawn Price.

"Dawn." I tried not to let his surprise enter my voice.

"I heard what you did for Max today."

I didn't respond to that. I felt as if I had a limited amount of words left today and didn't want to waste them.

"Thank you. For helping him."

"You don't need to thank me. Anyone would have done it."

Dawn and I both knew that wasn't true, as made evident by the crowd of students who stood gawking at Max writhing in pain on the floor, instead of engaging.

"I might know what happened," she spoke meekly, looking down toward her feet. She was attractive, but she preferred to keep her face hidden behind the curtain of hair that constantly hung in front of her face, and the signature black hood that was always draped over her head. I always felt like Dawn was shrouded in shadows, not just in the way she presented herself, but deep down to her very core.

"Like what drugs he took?" I asked. She nodded. "You should call the hospital. They could really use that information to help him."

"He called it 'The Sickness.'" She hugged her arms tightly around herself.

My brow furrowed.

The Sickness.

I was pretty ingrained in the world of local drugs, but that one was not ringing any bells. I made a mental note to speak to Jace tonight. She reached down into her tan cross body satchel and pulled out a journal. "This is his. He talks about this new drug that's been going around at the local college and how he finally got his hands on it." She spoke so quietly, I almost had to lean in to hear her.

"How do you have his journal?"

She recoiled slightly.

Interesting.

"I got it from his locker. I wanted to see if it had any clues as to what happened. And it did. Listen, I know you don't owe him, or me anything, but I don't even know where to start with this. I figured if anyone might be able to make sense of this, it would be you." She was right. My position in the school and the community at large was the one with the connections to the drug world. It was my birthright, I guess. I wasn't very proud of that.

"I'll look into it. Thanks."

She nodded before turning on her heel and heading towards the door.

"Wait, Dawn." I wasn't sure what possessed me, but at that moment I needed to say something to her. She turned around, offering no verbal response.

"You and Nani are pretty close, huh? I ran into them earlier. They were worried about you." Jealousy. Again. Instantly, I felt shame wash over me.

She seemed taken aback by that. As if I had just accused her of something horrendous. "I guess so." I could tell that was all the response I was going to get.

"I'll help Max. I promise."

She didn't say a word, but her eyes, heavy with sadness yet glimmering with a flicker of hope, followed me as she slipped out of the classroom. I stood there, trying to make sense of the strange encounter. Dawn was a puzzle I couldn't quite piece together, and with every new revelation, it only seemed to get more complicated. I found my gaze drifting down the hall, wondering what I'd missed.

A slight movement caught my eye, and I jerked slightly as Dawn's head reappeared from around a corner. A wave of recognition washed over me, like an echo from the past.

"Here's the journal. I'm not sure if it'll be useful, but... here." She tossed it to me, and I caught it without thinking. My mind scrambled to process what had just happened. The journal was another piece in the jumbled puzzle, but something more clicked into place as I held it.

Before I could fully grasp what was unfolding, a sharp memory cut through the fog of confusion. I'd seen that image before. Her delicate features peering out at me. Just this morning. Her face had been the one I'd glimpsed, not in a hallway, but through the ceiling tiles, watching the chaos with Max unfold below.

"Dawn Price..." I muttered under my breath, realization settling like a heavy weight in my chest. "Your puzzle just got a whole lot more interesting."

CHAPTER 5

PLAYERS GONNA PLAY

Friday night football games never appealed to me before. They still didn't now, but there was a good reason why I attended every Friday religiously, and it only partly had to do with seeing Brett Jacobs, number '12' in those unnecessarily, and pornographically tight pants. Friday Night football games were Jace's biggest nights. Under the bleachers he'd make nearly two hundred bucks off of teens looking to have a little fun, and I guess I fell into the role of right hand man a little too easily.

It was pretty chilly for an early Arizona October night, the fans were bundled in sweatshirts of blue and white, sporting the Falcons colors proudly. Some wore earmuffs and headbands that covered their heads while holding warm hot chocolate they got from the concession stand. I had to fight the scoff. If these people were freezing at seventy degrees, they would never survive up north.

I fantasized about it sometimes, leaving Arizona and starting over fresh somewhere up north. Far away from this town of people who only knew me as the boy whose parents chose drugs over him. Maybe I would, one day. Or maybe that was just a fantasy that someone like me could never achieve.

The student section was packed as I walked by, a sea of excited high schoolers with faces painted in vibrant colors and hair adorned with beads and pom poms. The cheerleaders were locked in a fierce call-and-response battle with the home bleachers, their chants blending together like a noisy argument, both sides competing to out-shout the other. From beneath the bleachers, the air was alive with the thunderous sound of feet stomping on the cold metal, as the cheerleaders worked the crowd into a frenzy.

I wore my normal outfit, black skinny jeans and leather jacket, but switched out my signature white tee for a tight blue shirt. Not that I was particularly filled with school spirit, but the cops that roamed the area were more likely to be suspicious of someone who wasn't in school colors. Jace was a lacrosse player, so he got away with wearing his letterman jacket. Between the two of us, we looked like regular old fans. But the steady stream of classmates coming to score a little fun served as a reminder to me that, no matter how much I wished for it, I wasn't a regular eighteen-year-old kid. I never would be. I sighed, watching the care-free students in the stands, laughing, cheering, and enjoying their evening as if they had nothing else to worry about in life.

I made my way out from under the bleachers and stood at the fence by the thirty yard line and for the first time that night, let myself watch the game, or more importantly, the players. Number '12' was the running back, and he was good. One of the best in the state according to a google search I performed before the first game of the season. Apparently my little jab that Brett had a scholarship waiting for him, was not entirely false. While he hadn't signed anywhere yet, there were already plenty of schools hoping to woo him into their program. Good for him. I guess.

I watched for a moment more, allowing myself to fully appreciate the fluidness of Brett's run, the strength in each step, the grace in which he dodged the oncoming tacklers. He sure was something. "Get a grip" I muttered before turning around, bumping directly into someone as they walked towards the bleachers.

"You've got to be freaking kidding me." Nyx Channery seethed. Nyx was a brick house of a human being. They towered over me at at least 6'5", and they had the muscle to back up every inch of that height. They wore dark colors tonight, which complimented their darker skin tone. Shaggy black hair hung in waves to their chin, unkempt and disorderly.

"Fuck. Sorry. I swear I'm not doing this on purpose," I muttered as I ran my hand through my hair. Of course this would happen. This tower of a human was going to kill me one day.

"You have a problem or something, Andras?" Nyx was accompanied by Salem Bridges and Dawn Price. Interesting combo, I thought. Nyx seemed fired up. Salem smiled devilishly at me while Dawn avoided eye contact. I couldn't help but let my eyes linger on Dawn, still reeling from what I pieced together this afternoon. None of it made any sense, but I knew what I saw. Just wasn't sure what it meant yet.

"Nyx, love. He didn't mean it. Right Kieran." The way Salem said my name made my face burn hot, and I was reminded of the hold she had on me in the hallway. She certainly had an interesting ability to entrance people.

"Three times this week. We're well past coincidence." Nyx's voice seemed to deepen, their eyes darkening almost inhumanly. My eyes squinted at them.

"Listen, I said I was sorry. I meant it. I have no idea why this keeps happening." Every time I looked at Nyx Channery I got this overwhelming feeling that they were dangerous and it was best not to cross them. The hairs on the back of my neck stood on end, and a chill trailed down my spine as their eyes bore into mine.

"Nyx." Dawn's soft voice somehow cut through the noise of the roaring crowd. Nyx's eyes lightened and their forehead muscles relaxed. They turned back and smiled shyly at Dawn before moving away from me without another word. Dawn shrugged at my inquisitive look and followed after, leaving only Salem and I behind.

"You've made a powerful enemy," she cooed. How she was able to make a threatening statement sound so damn sexy was beyond me.

"Wouldn't be the first time," I responded before I could catch myself. I thought back to the conversation I had earlier with my Angel. 'Enemy' was a strong word, but after today I certainly wasn't sure if I trusted him the way I used to, and that realization had me feeling adrift.

"You're always looking for trouble aren't you?" Salem smiled seductively.

"And you're running with a different crowd tonight."

She laughed. "Apparently Nyx's got themselves a little crush." Matters of the heart seemed to appeal to Salem. I wouldn't be surprised if she could smell desire a mile away. Seems like she popped up wherever there was romantic drama.

"On you?" I teased. Salem smiled brightly, like a damn bombshell. I usually wasn't this affected by such convention-ally attractive people, but Salem was a different story. Her angular features and hourglass frame were so alluring that it was almost as if she was specifically designed to be everyone's fantasy woman. I once again found myself imagining indulging in the desires she elicited in me.

"Not this time." She wore a tight blue knit cap that covered her ears and landed just above her perfectly manicured eyebrows. She wore a long sleeve white shirt under a blue puffy zip-up vest with the school logo embroidered. I had never spent a night with Salem, or an afternoon in a closet which seems to be my calling card as of late. But who knows, maybe now that Brett was out of the picture, I would be able to pursue different options. "I caught them looking at Dawn like she was some kind of runway model, which she definitely could be. Have you seen her cheekbones?" I had seen them, poking out of the ceiling tiles, but Salem didn't need to know that. "Anyway, I did what any good friend would do and introduced them."

"Are you actually friends with either of them?" Salem was a social butterfly, never sitting at the same lunch table two days in a row. But I'd never seen her with either of them before.

"I will be." And with a quick wink she was gone, strutting up the bleachers, her hips swaying with each step. I smiled after her, glad that I hadn't given into the temptation to pull her behind the bleachers and kiss her senseless, no matter how good it would have been. Now that she was out of my sight, I shook my head again. It was so weird how blindingly drawn to her I felt whenever she was around. She made her way to her friends and plopped down beside them. Maybe this would be good for Dawn.

My thoughts drifted back to her, what I'd seen, what she asked of me. I took one last look back on the field at number '12' just in time to see him getting tackled by a mountain of a man from the other team. The crowd erupted in a loud gasp.

"Serves you right." I said, but when my heart constricted with worry, I knew I didn't mean it. Maybe one day I would.

I was about to head back toward Jace when I heard an angry voice beside me.

"I told you not to fucking wear that."

The hair on the back of my neck stood on end and I felt a fury-filled chill wash over me as I turned toward the source of the voice.

An older guy, probably mid to late twenties at least, with greasy hair, and beady little rat eyes was staring down at a girl. I moved a little closer to see that it was Hannah, the girl who'd helped me with Max. She cowered at his words, her whole body folding in on itself. She was trying to make herself seem smaller. She was afraid of him. I felt my blood boil and I was rushing over toward them before I could even stop myself.

"Hannah," I said, drawing the man's attention away from her. "Nice to see you."

I was hoping she'd look relieved, happy that I had stepped in to draw his attention, but her wide eyed gaze looked terri-fied, her eyes flicking back and forth between the two of us.

"Who the hell is this, Hannah?" Douchebag McGee said, stepping forward till he was nearly toe to toe with me.

"Just someone in my class, John," she replied, meekly.

John.

A basic bitch name for a basic bitch.

I looked back to Hannah, who was pleading with me with her eyes. Shit. I think I just made this worse for her.

"Yeah," I said, backtracking carefully. "Barely know her," I tried to sound nonchalant, but the fury in John's eyes didn't dissipate. "Just wanted to thank her for helping that kid earli-er." I turned my gaze to her. "Not many people would have stepped up and helped, in fact most of them didn't. It was really cool of you to help him like that."

"Help who?" John butted in. His hand gripped her upper arm hard, pulling her attention to him.

"Whoa, calm down, dude. Get your hands off of her," I said, and instantly felt the mood shift. Hannah's terror seemed to intensify as John's anger ramped up.

"Who the fuck do you think you are telling me how I can and cannot touch my girlfriend?" His slimy voice seethed. I flicked my eyes toward Hannah, fully ready to smack down this asshole if she gave me the go ahead. But instead, she shook her head slowly, deliberately, pleading with me silently.

I sighed.

"Some kid was overdosing in the hallway at school, she stepped in to help," I said, trying to calm the situation down, despite the warnings in my head that told me to slam this asshole's face into the ground.

"Let's go, Hannah," John said, dragging her behind him. Her face looked so dejected, I had to compose myself to avoid running after them as they slipped into the crowd.

"That guy is a certified twat," a voice said from behind me. I turned to see Callum leaning against the fence, his eyes also trailing after Hannah and John.

"I should have beat him the hell up," I admitted, leaning my forearms on the fence beside him, barely handling the guilt that was swirling in my chest.

"I woulda helped ya," he agreed. "Fellas like him are dangerous."

I hated to agree with him. My eyes trailed after the pair again. Did I just make things worse for her? Was he going to take his anger with me out of her?

I felt my fists clench.

"We'll keep an eye on her, you and me," Callum stated. I turned to glance at him.

"We will?"

"Yeah, we'll form our own little... Hannah task force. We'll check in on her, make sure she's doin' grand," he said, resolved.

I let the idea dance in my mind.

"Yeah, ok," I agreed.

"And if he lays one more ungentle hand on her, we'll take him down. That is a promise I am more than willing to make," he declared, a mischievous glint in his eyes.

"Well, I better be off. I'm quite fascinated by the concept of American Football," he offered before skipping away. I watched after him for a moment before turning my attention back to the crowd where Hannah and John disappeared. When I couldn't find them immediately, I felt my chest constrict with guilt and fear.

Finally, I located them near the concessions. To my relief, he seemed to simply be ignoring her. I was thankful that Callum had thought of the idea to keep an eye on her. She was one of the only people who cared enough to step up when someone needed help, and I'd do the same for her.

After a while, I pushed through the crowd of middle schoolers and found my way back to Jace who had taken a seat on one of the concrete blocks under the bleachers and was discreetly counting a small wad of cash in his hand.

"You make quota?"

Jace jumped as I spoke behind him.

"Dude, you can't sneak up on a guy like that!" He stuffed the cash into the pocket of his jeans and turned back to me with a smile on his face. "And hell yes we did. Your whole 'homecoming special' idea was genius."

I nodded.

"People love a good deal." My mind was elsewhere. I didn't know how much Jace knew about the local drug scene, most of the time I was the one in the loop and Jace just took what Bryce gave him and went. But maybe he heard something. It was the only lead I had.

"Hey, Jace. Have you ever heard of something called The Sickness?" Instinctively, I lowered my voice. Jace looked at me with what appeared to be recognition. Perfect, I thought.

"That's the new Xbox game, right? Looks tight!" Ah. Ok.

"No." I shook my head, fighting a laugh. "It's a new type of drug going around. I thought maybe your brother might have told you about it."

"Told him about what?" The tone of Bryce's voice wasn't inherently threatening, but it definitely had an unsettling quality. Like you couldn't quite trust the words he was saying. I turned to face him, a taller, leaner version of Jace for sure. His hair was boxed dyed black, instead of its original sandy blonde. I hadn't seen him since he graduated. The summer had definitely changed him. Bryce used to fit into the world of drug dealing the way a child fits into their father's large t-shirt. Barely, and uncomfortably. But now, the person who stood before me looked dangerous, confident and definitely found his place within the world of ill repute. It was unnerving. He'd traded in his own letterman jacket that used to be his signature look, much like his brother's, for a red flannel over dark jeans and a black shirt.

"Bryce. Long time. How are you?" I spoke first. The corner of Bryce's mouth turned up in a smirk.

"Kieran. Still doing Jace's job for him?" Jace turned pale, and still had not spoken. Bryce stepped forward to me and settled his gaze on my face. "You know you can always come deal for me, get your own cut of it. Leave my pathetic brother to do his own work."

"Thanks, but I'm good. I told myself I'd never benefit from drugs again. Financially or otherwise." I was sober. He knew that. But I got the feeling that he didn't care.

"You still sitting around in a circle of freaks and crying on each other's shoulders?" He teased. I shot him a tight smirk.

He meant my NA meetings.

The first time I went to a Narcotics Anonymous meeting it was a cooler day for early September in Arizona. I remember needing my leather jacket not for fashion, but for actual warmth. I stood outside a musty old beige colored church. The one story building had a roofing issue, half of the shingles were flying off, and half of the roof was covered with a large blue tarp that looked like it was tied down by rope. As I stepped inside, buckets were scattered across the floor to collect the dripping moisture from the water damaged ceiling tiles. As I continued my walk down the hall, I was greeted by the smell of old wood. I couldn't imagine this being a place that was supposed to help me 'heal.'

I eventually reached the meeting room. The chairs had been arranged in a circular shape and most of them were already filled. Ten other hopeless cases occupied the seats and turned their heads to me as I approached. A middle aged bald man with small golden wire frame glasses sitting on the brim of his nose. His blue button shirt was tucked in nicely to his light khaki pants.

"Hey! Welcome. You're just in time. Have a seat." Too late to turn back now, I noted as I sat down in one of the open chairs. The faces slowly turned away and back towards the bald man. I knew it was impossible for a circle to have a "head of the table" that was the whole point behind the King Arthur thing, but this bald man was clearly exuding "head of table" energy as he smiled at all of the junkies sitting around him.

"Joshua, you were just about to tell us about your week." He prompted, and an older man, probably mid forties I guessed, although his skin looked wrinkled and weathered, stood up and nodded.

"Ok. Well. Hi, I'm Joshua and I'm a drug addict." I had to physically stop myself from groaning at the cliche of it all. "A few months ago I reached four years sober." I scanned the man's face, he looked tired, worn. Four years. That was impressive. Joshua paused and sighed, a few tears streamed down his face. "But two months ago, an old friend of mine from back when I was... well you know. She came into town, she wanted to say hi. I told her on the phone I didn't think it was a good idea. But she insisted she didn't have anything with her."

I knew where this was going, and according to the looks on the others' faces, they did too.

"So, we met up for coffee. It was really nice at first. But then she told me about this new club that she was in town for the opening. And I was enjoying her company so much that I decided to go with her." Tears were flowing down his face now. I felt a wave of understanding rush over me. If it's this hard after four years... how the hell am I going to do this for the rest of my life?

You have something they do not. Me.

My Angel cooed into my ear. I smiled. He was right. I felt relief and relaxation flood my body stemming from his warmth.

"What happened then, Joshua?" The bald man urged because clearly, aggressively forcing someone to talk about their trauma is a great plan. I hated this man already.

Joshua's sobs had overcome him. He held his head in his hands, his body was shaking. "It was one line. One single line. And it ruined everything." Ah, a cokehead. Joshua was lucky though, between all the drugs you could have fallen back into, coke wasn't too bad.

"It takes a lot of strength to resist our temptations, and it takes even more to admit when we have not been able to."

Bald Man, I decided I didn't care what his real name was, reached for Joshua's hand and nodded solemnly to him.

"But today, I have something for you."Bald Man handed Joshua a small token, about the size of a poker chip. I knew what it was and couldn't stop myself from letting out a short incredulous laugh. The heads in the room snapped towards me.

"Excuse me Mr..." Bald Man said. Oh shit. I didn't mean to do that.

"Kieran." I felt the stares of the other participants angrily bearing into me. Damnit.

"Was there a reason you mocked this huge moment in Josh's life?" All eyes were on me. Great.

"Ok. Well, yeah, actually. There was." This is going to be a mess. "Listen, Josh, you got to four years. That's massive. How the hell does a two-month chip make you feel any better after that? Isn't it just a slap in the face? Like congratulations for fucking up? If it were me, I wouldn't want one again until four years and one month. Something to work toward." The room was silent. Even Bald Man was shocked by my declaration.

"He's right. I don't want this. I'll wait until it's the one I need. The one I *will* get again." Bald Man had a shocked look on his face, but the other group members smiled and clapped for Joshua who had wiped his tears and smiled brightly.

Once the applause settled and Joshua had sat down, leaving Bald Man with the two-month chip in his hand, he spoke. "Well, then. Perhaps we can move on to you then." Bald Man moved to sit down again, he wasn't outwardly seething, but I knew silent rage when I saw it.

"Alright. Hi, I'm Kieran and I was a drug addict." They did not respond with their usual reply. Instead, they all turned their heads to Bald Man.

"Tell me why you used past tense there, Kieran." I didn't like the tone he used. The accusatory, derogatory tone made me feel like I was on trial.

"Because I'm not addicted anymore." A few of the other group members had turned to each other and began whispering.

"When's the last time you used?" Bald Man spoke again. This time he cooed as if talking to a child. I was pissed.

"Are you even allowed to ask me that?"

"I can ask, but you don't have to answer if you're uncomfortable being truthful." Fuck this guy. I felt hot, and warm, like a fire was burning inside of me.

Let them believe you are fragile. Let them believe you need their help. They don't deserve to know you have me.

I sighed.

"Two weeks ago." The murmurs continued.

"So, why the past tense?" Bald Man leaned forward and I wanted to sock him in the jaw, but decided to listen to my Angel, who always knew best.

"Call it wishful thinking, I guess." I didn't need to tell them that I had a new strength from something bigger than myself. I didn't need to tell them that drugs aren't appealing to me anymore. That temptation was non-existent.

"Well. I think it's noble that you are looking forward to what you hope for yourself. And it is also important to understand where we are now." I decided that Bald Man was divorced with three estranged kids who chose to live with the other parent over him because this insufferable asshole was impossible to handle.

"Yeah."

"What made you decide it was time to get sober?" I thought about that for a moment. I knew the surface-level answer was that my Angel told me to give it up, but there was more to it.

"Someone told me I was worth saving, so I believed them."

I went to Narcotics Anonymous every week, religiously. Bald Man's name is really Ted, and he was actually a pretty great listener. However, he gives a painfully awful first impression. A fact I told him about, in depth, when he gave me my sixth month chip. I knew I didn't need that support system, because I already had my own, but it felt nice to be among others who felt the same. Joshua still hasn't accepted a chip. He's holding out for four years and one month.

"Waste of time if you ask me," Bryce stated matter of factly, snapping my attention back to him.

I shrugged, not really interested in getting into it.

"You know, offer's still open, Andras." I wasn't sure if he actually wanted my help or if he just wanted to pour some salt on Jace's wound.

"Thanks, but I'm good."

Bryce shrugged and then turned back to his brother who was making himself smaller by gripping his arms tightly around him.

"What are you doing here, Bryce? I told you I was gonna make quota on my own." Bryce smiled and arched his eyebrow.

"Was it? On your own, I mean?" He tilted his head towards me and Jace pulled his jacket tighter around himself. "Listen, I'm not here to babysit you, I'm here on my own business."

Jace nodded but didn't respond.

"Have anything to do with this Sickness I'm hearing about?" I blurted. If anyone would know, it's Bryce, and honestly, I wasn't afraid of the scrawny low-time dealer in front of me. He may look the part of a sleazy, badass dealer

now, but I knew him long before the box dye, and the hard-
ened shell. He was nothing more than a pathetic weasel.

"Who's talking about it?" He replied with an edge in his
voice. Ok. Progress.

"Does that matter?" I raised an eyebrow in challenge.
Bryce didn't like to be pushed. But neither did I. At least not
unless it had sex involved.

"Let's just say we're trying something new." Bryce eventually spoke. His tongue grazed over his top teeth slightly as he
smiled and his shoulders shook as if he was laughing at some
inside joke that no one understood.

I thought for a long moment about how I wanted to
play this. I could be forceful, Bryce was an antagonist,
maybe he would respond to force? Or I could sweet talk
him, Bryce also has an ego the size of New York City so that
could be a good approach. Or I could trigger his fear. He
may talk a big game, but I know he doesn't want to get
caught.

"Yeah well your 'new thing' is starting to cause waves, in all
the wrong ways." Bryce's eyebrow raised. Good. He's listening.

"How so?" His face was calm. If he was worried about
what information I had, he didn't let on. His douchey smirk
remained plastered on his lips.

"Someone OD'd in the hall at school. And it didn't look
like a regular OD. Whatever you're cutting right now, it's
different and it's gonna be easy to trace." I tried to keep my
voice steady, but I was right. Whatever this stuff was, it wasn't
like anything else out there right now. The effects are pretty
visible, and that green ooze shit is gonna be analyzed eventually. Hell, Bryce is lucky no one's been banging down his door
already.

Bryce absorbed the information and nodded as his eyes
drifted to the ground, his smirk never faltering, but his shoul-

ders tensing up told me all I needed to know. His eyes turned dark for a second as he whispered.

"I'll be sure to let him know." He turned on his heel and took off toward the parking lot.

"Well, that's the first time I've ever seen Bryce run away with his tail between his legs." Jace gawked after him. I also noted how strange that reaction was. Bryce was not the type to run scared. Nor was he the type to be so sloppy.

"Who's the 'him' he was talking about?" I asked, not taking my eyes off Bryce until he disappeared behind crowds of people in the parking lot.

"No idea. He's not living at home anymore."

My eyes snapped to Jace.

"Since when? He was still there this summer wasn't he?" Not that it mattered, but puzzle pieces were puzzle pieces.

"A month ago now? He met some friends in his chemistry class and apparently they wanted to room together. Maybe one of them is who he's talking about?" Jace nonchalantly took out a rolled joint from his pocket and lit it. I rolled my eyes. Meeting another drug dealer in chemistry class? What a damn cliche.

"Maybe." I turned back in the direction that Bryce left. What am I missing? "What's his address?"

"Hell if I know."

"He's your brother."

"So?"

I scoffed, balling my fists at my side. "Hey, I gotta run, I'll be back soon alright. If you don't hear from me though I probably just went home." I didn't wait for Jace's response before I took off jogging toward the parking lot. Brushing past parents and middle schoolers, I had one target in mind and I had to act fast.

There he was. Bryce had stopped in the parking lot about thirty yards from his car. I spent quite a few evenings getting high in that backseat a year and a half ago. I looked at the person standing near Bryce. Rhonda. Her red hair was pulled back in two even french braids and her cheeks were painted with blue and white designs. She smiled at Bryce and her fingers played with the end of her braids. Bryce didn't seem super into it, but enough that I had a moment. Just a moment.

I slid my phone out of my pocket and turned it on silent. No vibrate, nothing. Alarms off. Good. I double checked it then slid through the shadows toward Bryce's car. Rhonda had moved closer to him, I could see her hands slowly grazing the front of his thighs. He'd be distracted, but probably not for long. I surveyed the vehicle. Windows were up. Damn. I ran my fingers through my hair. I was banking on a cracked window. I looked around again, my eyes glued on the back of Bryce's head as I reached for the door handle. Locked.

'Shit," I cursed. I had one chance to execute this plan. And it all hinged on this car being unlocked.

CLICK

I jumped as the sound of the locked disengagement startled me. "Fuck," I whispered and quickly looked back to Rhonda and Bryce. Their lips were locked in a heated make out session and Bryce was stepping backwards toward his car, Rhonda stumbling forward as they fought to keep their lips together. I smiled before quickly opening the passenger door, Bryce and Rhonda none the wiser as they continued their passionate stumble to the car. As I opened the door slightly, I was greeted with the overwhelming aroma of weed. I paused. God, that's familiar. Back when it was simple, back before it got too hardcore. Sometimes I wish I could indulge in those "gateway drugs". But I don't need them anymore. I have something better.

Had.

Have.

Shit.

Still need to think about that.

I slipped my phone under the passenger seat and tucked it beneath a pair of shorts that had probably been sitting back here for years. Once I was sure it was securely placed, I shut the door lightly and slid away into the night. I watched as Bryce and Rhonda toppled into the backseat and held my breath waiting for Bryce to notice, to see something was off... But he didn't. I turned away as Bryce was ripping off Rhonda's shirt.

I smiled to myself as my plan started taking root.

"You're ridiculous, dude." Jace had said one weekend over summer.

"Thanks. Now, will you just help me look?" I walked with my back hunched as I slowly surveyed the ground at my feet. The walking trail in the state park is a mile and a half long. And we had just walked it all.

"I can't lose my phone," I said, a slight air of desperation echoing in my tone. I could barely afford my rent, let alone a new phone.

"Just use Find My Phone." Jace had taken up residence on a large boulder that sat on the edge of the trail and leaned, the back of his head cradled in his hands.

"What?" I stood.

"Find My Phone. You put music on your phone using your computer right?" I nodded. "Then you can use Find My Phone on your computer to track your phone." I dropped my black backpack quickly and pulled out my hand-me-down laptop I got at a pawn shop. Jace spent the next twenty minutes showing me how to work the application and within moments, we found my phone.

As I walked away from Bryce's car, I knew I'd be able to find my phone again soon enough, and with any luck... The Sickness too.

CHAPTER 6
DRUG WATCH

THE GAME ENDED in favor of the Falcons, and the stadium was alight with electric energy, but as the satisfied fans and eager players began filing out of the Cactus Shadows High School Football field, I sat atop a picnic table, anxiously waiting for the night to end so that I could search for my phone and get some answers.

I saw Nyx Channery moving toward the exit and instantly tensed up. There was something so...feral about them, it made my usual bravado falter when in their presence. Not to mention, after this week, I was headed right for a lashing out.

Salem winked at me as she passed by, and I couldn't help the smirk that lifted my lips. My eyes landed on Dawn, who walked quietly at Nyx's side. Her head was down, looking at her feet as they hit the ground. Nyx's hand dangled purpose-fully close to Dawn's empty hand. My eyes watched as their fingers gravitated toward each other.

The moment Nyx's hand brushed against Dawn's flesh, she smiled. Actually smiled. I could practically feel Salem's triumph from here.

The three of them headed toward the parking lot, and

Dawn's eyes landed on me. She said something to Salem and Nyx before jogging across the lot to where I sat. I felt Nyx's gaze on me, jealousy, anger, hatred... you name it, they felt it.

Dawn came to a stop before me, I raised an eyebrow. "You're going to get me killed," I joked, and Dawn's face paled. Any remnants of her smile were long gone. "Hey, sorry. I just meant..." I stumbled off of the picnic table, standing in front of her. "Nyx over there looks a little territorial. Seems like they've got the hots for you and are not interested in sharing with me."

Dawn's eyes widened, and a blush crept across her face.

"They.. um... No, it's not like that..we're just.." She rambled. I smirked, her innocence was refreshing.

"Hey, you don't have to explain anything to me. I suck at relationships." I tossed my hands up, feigning a laugh just as a group of football players exited the locker room door. The door that I had, completely coincidentally of course, a perfect view from this spot. Brett Jacobs led his teammates out into the night, where they were met with a smattering of applause from fans who had stayed to congratulate them. He was beaming, proud of his performance. Then his eyes landed on me. A delicious, promising heat passed through his gaze, but I wasn't all that interested in being burned anymore. I sighed before tearing my eyes from him and looking back at the seemingly fragile girl before me. But something told me that Dawn Price was anything but fragile.

"Did you find anything out about...The Sickness?" She asked, leaning in to whisper the words to me. I looked over my shoulder to ensure that nobody could hear us.

"Not much, but I have a good lead that I'm going to follow tonight."

She nodded, absorbing my words.

"Can I come?"

My eyes flicked up to see Salem and Nyx, standing a couple of dozen yards away, Salem trying to hold a conversation with the tall and intimidating figure, while their eyes bore into my soul.

"Not sure your guard dog would allow that," I teased. Dawn winced.

"Nyx knows why I came to talk to you." It was my turn to look shocked. "I didn't tell them much, just that you were helping me figure out what Max took." A shiver echoed through my body.

"Keep it that way," I snapped. "This shit is dangerous and we can't take any chances of people knowing we're onto them."

"Them?" Dawn asked, her face colored with worry. I sighed, and ran a hand through my hair.

"You wanna come with me?"

She nodded, and I battled with myself for a few moments internally. This wasn't safe, not even for me. Definitely not for Dawn Price.

Let her come.

The familiar voice shocked me, sending a wave of fear coursing through my veins instead of the calming effect it normally had.

"Okay, we'll leave in a few minutes." I said, tossing my gaze briefly back to the football players who were entertaining their fans. Students who saw these athletes every single day in school were acting as if they were in the presence of fucking royalty on Friday nights. I used to laugh about it with Brett after the game, when he would come to my studio and celebrate his victory by screaming my name.

"I'll just let Salem know that I'm getting a ride with you," she said, taking a few steps back. I smiled down at Dawn.

"Be sure to tell Nyx that I'll keep my hands to myself," I

teased. Dawn rolled her eyes before turning completely and bounding back to her friends.

"You enjoy the game?" Brett's low voice sounded from behind me. It was deep and gravely from an evening of yelling and cheering. Sexy as fuck, is what it was. I closed my eyes, taking a deep breath to compose myself before turning to face him.

His brown skin was shining with perspiration, and I had to force my eyes not to scan his body.

"Did you win?" I asked. It was a cheap shot, but hell, if I was going to stay strong here, I was gonna need to fight dirty.

"Sure did." He smiled, pride oozing from his pores. I hated how fucking alluring he could be when he was riding a high like this.

"Good for you," I exclaimed, quietly. We stood facing each other in silence for a moment.

"I wish I could celebrate." His voice was low, full of promises that I knew he wasn't ready to keep. I sighed, angry that my body was reacting to his words.

"I'm sure Ashley would be willing to oblige," I said, through gritted teeth. He rolled his eyes.

"Admit it, you miss me," he said, taking a single step forward. He was now only five or so feet from me, but I felt his body calling to mine from across the expanse.

"I wouldn't want to lie to you," I spat. His eyes burned.

"Kieran, I need you," he whispered. I placed my hand to my ear and leaned forward.

"I'm sorry, I couldn't hear you, what did you say?" It was a cruel game, but one I was more than willing to play.

He took another step toward me, his eyes scanning his surroundings. "You heard me loud and clear, and you know it."

I scoffed.

"Kieran, I need you," he said again, his voice a breathly plea. My length strained against my jeans as it responded to his begging. His eyes flicked down and his tongue darted out to lick his lip as he saw evidence of what he was doing to me.

"Need me to do what, Brett?" I asked.

He looked around again, ensuring we were alone before responding. "I need you to make me scream, Kieran."

A moan escaped my lips and suddenly my jeans felt like they were two sizes too small. "Brett... I.." I took a single step forward, nearly ready to give everything up for this one night.

"There you are!" The loud, cheery voice pulled me from the tense fantasy we created. Brett cleared his throat and took a step back as his girlfriend, Ashley, tossed her arms around his neck.

I shook my head, ashamed that I had been so close to giving in to that temptation. Again.

"Hey, Ash." Brett's hand found its resting spot on Ashley's ass, and I rolled my eyes to mask the pain.

"You ready to go home?" She asked, her words oozing with subtext.

"Yeah, Brett, you should go celebrate," I said, with a sickly sweet taunt, he narrowed his eyes in warning and Ashley turned to look at me.

I didn't notice the small frame that had come to a stop beside me until I saw Ashley's eyes flick toward her. I turned to see Dawn, head down, avoiding eye contact with Ashley.

"Andras. Price. I'm going to steal my boyfriend now," she cooed. I felt my heart pound against my chest, as she kissed his exposed neck.

"He's all yours," I said, willing as much nonchalance as I could muster.

"Have a great time you two," she teased with ample innuendo, her eyes bouncing between us.

I turned to Dawn, analyzing the shut-down look on her face before tossing my arm around her shoulder. I really fucking hope Nyx has already left.

Dawn didn't even acknowledge my arm on her as I went to pull her away.

"See ya," I tossed over my shoulder at the two of them. Ashley's eyes bore into the back of Dawn's head with a vicious type of resentment. And when I turned to see Brett, his eyes were full of jealousy. Good. See how it feels.

I led Dawn to my car, opening the passenger door for her and helping her in. She was quieter than even her normal quiet. It was unnerving. Easing into the car, I gripped the steering wheel tightly.

"I just need to stop by my apartment and check my computer for the coordinates, and then we can be on our way," I said, desperately wishing my heart rate would return to a normal rate. Her eyes were trained on her folded hands. Her soft brown hair fell down in a curtain in front of her. I think she would disappear if she could.

It wasn't my place to ask her what's wrong, was it?

You could help her.

I shook the voice from my mind. The last thing I was going to do was be intimate with Dawn Price.

I guess, talking to her was the only option. Either that or sit in uncomfortable silence. The car revved as I pulled out of the parking lot and turned toward my apartment.

"Everything okay?" I asked, forcing an air of nonchalance.

"What?" Her head popped up, her brown eyes were wide and worried. "Oh, um, I'm fine."

She's lying.

'I know.' I bit back at the whisper in my head. How had I never questioned him before?

I can help you see.

Shaking my head, I turned my eyes toward the frightened woman in my car. I wish she would tell me herself what's wrong. I didn't want to pull it from her. But if she was this afraid of something, it might be important for me to find out what it is.

'Fine. Help me.'

That's what I'm here for, boy.

My vision blurred, a deep red haze overtaking everything like a storm of fire and brimstone. My Angel's presence tightened its grip on my mind, pulling me into the depths of his power, far deeper than I'd ever dared to go before. Suddenly, I wasn't in the car anymore. But I was still with Dawn.

This dream version, however, was different, calm, content... happy, even. A stark contrast to the one sitting beside me in the real world. Her phone buzzed, shattering the serenity of the dreamscape. That's when everything shifted. Darkness surged in, fear, anger, shame, and a tidal wave of raw emotion. Dawn screamed, hurling her phone across the room. I nearly reached out to comfort her before remembering this wasn't real. It was a memory.

I moved toward where her cracked phone had landed. The screen flickered with a frozen image. The tape. The very tape that had torn through the school like wildfire.

You know who did this, right?

I shook my head, averting my eyes from the frozen screenshot of vulnerable intimacy on the screen.

Ashley.

My breath caught in my throat. Of course. Saying that Ashley Harris could be a bitch was a severe understatement, but I never thought she would go this far.

I turned back to the broken girl lying in a heap on the floor. Her arms circling her, holding herself together as if her soul was nothing but shattered empty pieces on the floor. The edge of my gaze began to soften, slowly slipping away. The insistent buzz of her phone dragged my eyes from her form.

Texts, and calls flooded in, painting the cracked screen. One name repeated, again and again.

> MAX: Dawn.. did you see it?

> MAX: Please call me...

> MAX: I can't believe this.

> MAX: Maybe nobody's seen it.

> MAX: I'm sorry.

The red cloud finished its possession of my vision and suddenly my eyes refocused on the road ahead. A dull song played over the radio, and I could hear Dawn's quiet breathing next to me.

"Ashley Harris is a shitty person," I said, lacing my tone with disdain. She turned to me, her eyes searching my face for an answer to a question I didn't know.

"I guess so." She shrugged. I gripped the wheel tighter still.

"You know, if you ever want to talk. I'm a pretty good listener, and I'm great at staying anonymous," I teased, but immediately cringed. Not that I cared, but I guess it displays a certain level of weakness that I'm actively in Narcotics Anonymous. Not that getting help is a weakness, but when people know things about you, they can exploit it. That's why I keep my secrets close. When I can.

But something told me I could trust Dawn.

"So, you're going through a lot to help Max, are you two..." I prompted. Her eyes widened and a blush darkened her face.

"What do you know?" It was an accusation, anger and fear coloring her expression. I shook my head.

"I know that Ashley's going nowhere in life, and I know that you didn't deserve to be the only one who took the heat for that video." A single tear escaped her eye, she wiped it quickly with the sleeve of her hoodie before turning from me.

"You didn't deserve to take heat at all, actually," I admitted. It was true. The double standard was disgusting. She was ridiculed, tormented, called unspeakable names all because she had sex. There was a brief, and annoying, time when people speculated it was me on the screen there with her, and instead of getting treated like a social pariah, I was offered high fives and congratulations. She should never have to feel ashamed for what she does in her spare time. "It's not fair what you went through."

She was crying fully now.

Shit. I didn't know what to do with a crying chick.

"Hey, I'm sorry. I'm not trying to pry into your life, Dawn. But I want you to know that you're justified in your anger." Her head tilted towards me again, her brown eyes glistening with unshed tears. "Toward both of them."

"What..."

"He didn't step up when you needed him. And that's a pretty shitty thing for Max to do." I didn't mean to let the name slip, but it had. I hoped she didn't ask because I wasn't in the mood to lie to her.

Tears fell freely, gliding across her pale skin leaving trails of moisture in their wake. "Kieran, I don't know how you know..." she started, sniffling. "But thank you."

I nodded, but didn't say a word. There was nothing else to say.

A few minutes later I pulled up in front of Shadow Acres

Apartment Complex. Parking the car, I quickly rolled up the windows and manually locked the door.

"You should come in with me," I urged, tense. She glanced out the window, looking at her surroundings. It wasn't much. Three one floor buildings, an old motel converted to low income living, a small park that hasn't seen new updates or additions since it was built in 1999.

"I can't wait here? How long are you going to be?" I sighed.

"Honestly, it'll only take a minute, but this isn't exactly the best neighborhood to just be... alone." I wasn't ashamed of my lot in life, but I did hate how she was looking at me now. Her eyebrows scrunched up as she studied me.

"But you live here..."

"I wish I didn't."

Her eyes softened as she took a deep breath.

"I'll be ok, I'd rather wait out here." She settled into her seat and I fought the urge to insist, and instead grabbed my keys.

"Keep the door locked, okay?" I said. She nodded and I sprinted toward my door. It was nearly pitch dark out here, save for the single flickering yellow street light that cast a blanket of eerie light across the parking lot, sending strange, stretching shadows dancing along the pavement.

I added a few extra locks to the door when I moved in, so I made quick work of releasing the three massive clasps. Slipping inside, I spied my small desk sitting in the corner with my laptop perched atop it. Opening the Find my Phone application, I tracked the small blue dot.

"Okay, where the hell are you, Bryce?"

The blue dot hovered over a small apartment building just outside of the local community college.

"Got you," I whispered, quickly scribbling the location onto a piece of scrap paper.

A minute later I was sliding back into the driver seat of the junk storm.

"Did you get what you needed?" Dawn asked, peering up at me through damp eyelashes. She had stopped crying, but the reminder of her pain was still present on her face.

"Yeah, I did." I pulled out of the parking lot, leaving my home behind. Dawn glanced back at my reality and sighed deeply. "Don't do that.." I warned, softly.

"Do what?" She asked, flipping her gaze back to me.

"Feel sorry for me." The car was quiet as my whispered plea hung in the air between us. Dawn's low steady breathing was the only sound permeating.

"Kieran, that's not..." she started, struggling to find the words she needed. "That's not what I was feeling." I flicked my eyes towards her for a moment, before returning them to the road ahead. "I don't pity you...I envy you."

My eyebrows furrowed and I found myself speechless. Dawn sighed as if she was frustrated that she even had to explain herself.

"I don't understand," I responded, incredulously. "I grew up in a nightmare and now I live alone in a shitty studio on the wrong side of town."

"At least you got out." Her raised voice echoed against the interior of the car. A pause. "You got to leave your nightmare, Kieran. Not everybody does."

We came to a stoplight and I fully turned to meet her gaze. Her eyes were not welling with tears as they had earlier, but instead, they burned with anger and fire.

She needs to be saved, Kieran.

I shut my eyes tightly, forcing my angel to the back of my mind. Once I was sure he was tucked safely behind my walls, I opened my eyes to find Dawn cast in a bright red haze from the stop light in front of us. She was right, of course. I was lucky. Even though it never felt like that.

Not many Judges rule in favor of emancipation, and not many jobs hire underage kids. I was lucky enough to get a steady enough income, good enough grades, and a damn good lawyer who was willing to work pro bono to help me get free of the shackles of my previous life.

Sometimes, I feel like I traded one shitty existence for another. But that's not true. Dawn's right. I was lucky.

"Are you okay, Dawn?" The light turned green and as I accelerated, I heard Dawn's breath falter.

"Can we just try to figure out what's wrong with Max?" She stated, effectively shutting down that particular thread of conversation.

Two months ago, if you had asked me if I ever thought I'd be worried about Dawn Price, I probably would have laughed at you. But right now, my heart constricted at the thought of her dealing with this situation alone.

"Okay, this is it," I said, pulling up in front of a large brick building with glass doors. A few people sat outside on the lawn in front of the building with drinks in their hands.

"What's your plan?" She asked, turning uncomfortably in her seat.

"I used to hang out with Bryce all the time, I'll just... pretend I'm there to buy." Dawn shook her head and put her hand on mine to stop me from getting out.

"You're sober, everyone knows that. He won't buy it." Damnit, she's right. Again. My tongue trailed across the front of my teeth as I thought.

"Maybe I can tell him I'm there to deal...he's been trying to get me to come back and work for him for months."

Dawn pursed her lips as she analyzed that idea. "What should I do?"

"My phone is in his car, that one right there." I pointed to Bryce's car in the parking lot. "Think you could see if it's unlocked. It's under the passenger seat."

She looked over at the vehicle and nodded. "Yeah, I can do that."

She slid out of the car and headed toward Bryce's vehicle. I locked the junk storm and carefully made my way up the sidewalk to the front doors. The few people who were enjoying a drink on the lawn barely looked my way as I passed them, too engrossed in their drink and their conversation to care about the skinny kid in a leather jacket. Good.

I had no idea which apartment was Bryce's but I did intimately know the scent of a drug dealer's apartment. Following my nose, I walked up a flight of stairs to the second floor. The dulled sounds of metal music drifted from beneath a door, and the scent of marijuana seeped into the hall.

"Fuck you!" The muffled scream echoed through the hallway. I'd heard Bryce pissed off enough to know the scream belonged to him. My feet came to a stop just outside the door. "You went and ran your mouth didn't you?!" I took a deep breath, hating the way the residual scent of marijuana felt on my tongue. It was a strange sensation, simultaneously detesting and aching for something.

"You're being paranoid," a second, more feminine voice chimed in. I strained to hear the quieter toned individual.

"I'm not being paranoid, Sarah! I'm telling you that people who shouldn't know about it, know about it." Bryce was pacing, I heard the shuffling of his feet from just beyond the door.

Sarah. Who the hell was Sarah?

"Calm down, it's almost time anyway, you don't need to

be such a douche about it." Almost time? What the hell were these two planning?

"He isn't going to be happy that you've been spilling our secrets for the whole damn town." I tried not to scoff at the fact that Bryce's loud mouthed rant could be heard clear as day from the hall. Chances are high, that if word *did* get out, it was more than likely his fault.

Also... who's *he?*

"Just do your part, and everything will be fine. We have the batch ready for tomorrow right?" I strained to hear the dulcet tones of Sarah's voice, trying to see if I recognized her.

"Of course everything's ready, I'm not a fucking idiot."

Sarah laughed.

"Then we've got nothing to worry about. This time tomorrow, it'll be too late for anyone to stop him, even if they wanted to. Those kids won't know what hit them." My heart leapt up into my throat. This didn't sound like a normal fucking drug ring, an eerie chill ran up my spine as I contemplated my next move.

I could knock, play the interested party and try to get "in" on the deal. Or I could get the fuck out, and leave this whole damn problem behind me.

Dawn's face flashed in my mind, sticking through the tile of the ceiling, which I still needed to talk to her about, but full of fear, and worry for her friend. I used to think that people that took drugs deserved whatever was coming to them, me included. But if whatever Bryce, Sarah and this secretive 'he' had planned was going to make a lot of people react the way Max had...then we had a problem. A huge problem. One I couldn't ignore.

You must stop them.

I felt the muscles in my neck tighten as his voice echoed in my mind. My hand absentmindedly rubbed the tanned skin above the collar of my jacket.

'Do you know what's going on here?' I asked the voice in my head. I waited only a moment for his response.

Of course, I do.

Had the angel always been so frustrating?

'Ok, will you tell me?' I asked, restraining the annoyance in my voice.

All you need to know is that you cannot let them succeed.

'I agree. But why are you so invested?'

You've been asking questions lately, Kieran. You wouldn't be starting to doubt my intentions...would you?

The last two words darkened, a sinister gruff shadowed behind his veiled threat. Damn, what had I gotten myself into?

'Of course not.'

Good.

I shook away the residual tension that came with my recent conversation with the angel. I was suddenly seeing things through a very different light. Analyzing old conversations. Replaying moments when I thought I was being saved... Did I give up one addiction for another?

The door handle to Bryce's apartment jiggled, promptly shaking me from my thoughts. I quickly ran down the flight of stairs, and hightailed it out the front door. The drinking neighbors didn't even glance my way as I fast walked to the junk storm. Dawn was already sitting back in my car. I pulled on the door handle to the driver side to find my car still locked, despite Dawn sitting inside of it. My eyebrows furrowed as I dug my keys out of my hand and unlocked the car.

I didn't have time to ask questions, not yet anyway. I slid into the driver's seat, turned the key and drove off. Tossing one look behind me, I couldn't see Bryce, so I sent a silent prayer to whatever God was out there and hadn't given up on me yet, that he hadn't seen me.

"I got your phone." Dawn said, holding up the device in her pale hands. I smiled, and reached for it.

"He left his car unlocked?" I asked, breathlessly. I saw her breath catch, and her hands began fidgeting in her lap once they were free of the phone.

Interesting.

Once I was positive we were far enough from Bryce's place, I pulled off the road into a gas station parking lot. Putting the car in park, I leaned my head back against the headrest and exhaled fully for the first time in what felt like hours.

"What did you find out?" she asked meekly from her spot. I recognized the diversion tactic and made a silent note to return to the current questions swimming in my mind once I told her about my discoveries.

"Not much, except that Bryce and some girl named Sarah are working for somebody else, some 'him,' and there's something going down tomorrow night." Dawn's eyes widened.

"Tomorrow is Homecoming, you don't think they'd do anything there?" Shit. I had forgotten all about the archaic school dance. A fuck ton of stupid high schoolers with hormones, no real experience with drugs, and a pocket full of allowances...

Sarah was right. Those kids won't know what hit them.

"Yeah, I do think."

Dawn ran her hands anxiously through her cropped brown hair. I watched her angular face, studying it intently.

"Dawn?" I asked. Her head tilted in my direction. The look on her face told me that she knew what I was about to ask wasn't a question she wanted to answer.

"Kieran," she answered slowly. I turned in my seat, the safety belt digging into my waist uncomfortably.

"Bryce's car wasn't unlocked was it?"

Her eyes remained plastered on mine. Her tongue ran across her bottom lip tentatively.

"No."

I nodded.

"And neither was mine," I added as if I was a detective at the end of the movie laying out the evidence to the culprit. She sighed.

"No, it wasn't."

"And I'm pretty sure I saw you poking your head through the ceiling at school." I tried not to let my voice shake, because what I was about to infer was crazy beyond belief, and yet it made perfect sense. Her eyes darted around my face in shock. She hadn't known I'd seen that. "So what is it? You can walk through walls?" I asked, fully aware of how ridiculous I sounded.

She opened her mouth to respond, but closed it tightly. She lifted her hand, hovered it over the dashboard, and then pushed through. Her hand disappeared into the plastic interior of my car as if her form hadn't just been entirely solid.

I had to remind myself to keep breathing.

"Holy shit," I whispered as she drew her hand back from the depths of my car's hood. Without thinking I reached out, taking her hand in mine. It felt cold to the touch, but it was there. Solid. Real.

"How?" I asked, my voice quiet.

When my eyes returned to her face, I saw the tears that were falling down her cheeks. I resisted the urge to pull away again.

"I'm dead Kieran."

CHAPTER 7

OH SHIT. THIS IS THE PART WHERE I START TO FEEL THINGS, ISN'T IT?

OF ALL THE things Dawn Price could have said, that wasn't even on my radar. Her hand stayed locked in mine as my eyes roved over her face, my gaze sweeping over every detail, trying to see the truth hidden in her words.

"What?" I asked, unable to hide my shock.

"I'm dead," she repeated, and still it felt wrong. "I died, but I'm still here."

Part of me wanted to laugh in her face, to tell her how ridiculous she sounded for making something like that up. It was impossible. It didn't make any sense. It couldn't be true... and yet. The other part of me felt compelled to believe that what she was telling me was the truth. No matter how unbelievable it was.

"When?" Because apparently one syllable words were all I was currently capable of at the moment. I watched her throat bob as she swallowed, her dark brown eyes glistening with tears as they poured freely.

"This summer. After..." Fuck. Her words hit me harder than any drug had before. My entire chest tightened as I put the jumbled puzzle pieces together. "I couldn't handle it anymore, Kieran." She didn't pull her hand back, but I felt her fingers tighten into a fist. My heart broke into a thousand pieces for the girl in front of me. I had heard the dark call of oblivion a few times myself, but to think of Dawn going through that, making that choice... something inside of me shattered.

And then, a darker thought crossed my mind.

No.

"The stuff you bought from me..." I didn't want to know. But I had to.

She nodded, averting her eyes.

Fuck.

Tears flowed down my own cheeks now, blurring the vision of the woman in my passenger seat. I pulled my hands from hers and slammed them into the steering wheel.

"Kieran..." her voice didn't reach me though. I was gone. I was lost.

"Fuck, Dawn. I'm so... I knew I shouldn't have... Damnit!" I wasn't making any sense. I knew that. I felt her hand rest on my shoulder. Somehow I'd put the burden of comforting me on her shoulders, how fucked up was that?

I turned back to her, wiping away the streaks of my breakdown from my cheeks.

"I don't blame you, Kieran," she whispered between gentle, broken sobs. She didn't need to blame me. I blamed myself.

You can fix this. You can fix her.

I jolted upright, my back stiffening.

'I've done enough.' I replied back through the channels of my mind.

I forced my angel - or maybe more appropriately, devil - to the back of my mind and took in Dawn's features. She was pale, paler than last year for sure. Was that a symptom of what-ever had happened to her?

"I'm so sorry, Dawn," I whispered, the very picture of a broken man. She nodded, tears slowing their path along her cheeks. "I checked on you, a few days after that day under the bleachers. I went to your house, I waited to make sure I saw you. Waited until I knew you were okay." I tried to make eye contact with her, but felt so unworthy of it. She tilted her head, taking in my words. "I should have said something."

"I don't know why I didn't... well, die, completely. I don't know why I'm still here, but I do know that I alone made that choice, Kieran." She was still trying to comfort me, and it pissed me off. She did not deserve to carry the burden of my shame. I squeezed her hand in mine.

"I'm glad you're here." Our eyes met and for a moment, I felt like maybe there was someone else who really understood me, really understood how painful life could be. And maybe we were both going to be okay.

"Can you drop me off at Nyx's?" Dawn said, changing the subject abruptly. I caught a quick glance of myself in my rearview mirror, admiring how the red rim around my blue eyes made them stand out.

"Booty call?" I asked, pointing to the clock on my dash-board. It was nearly 11:00 pm already.

Dawn's voice caught in her throat, and I tried to hide my smirk, thankful for the newfound levity. "They invited me to stay over with Salem earlier, they're both over there."

"So an orgy then," I teased and Dawn's hand smacked my shoulder quicker than I got the words out. I growled out a laugh.

"Stop!" She cried, but her laughter told me she appreciated the new line of conversation as much as I did. I pulled out onto the street.

"Salem would probably love that." I mused.

Dawn's smile deepened. Interesting.

"You'll have to direct me, I have no idea where Nyx lives. And I'm not sure they want me to anyway."

Dawn gave me directions, laughing periodically at my crude humor. It felt good to see her laugh, to watch her light up, despite everything she revealed to me tonight. Maybe that was how I could repent for what I did.

I found myself wondering if anyone else knew, or if she had only felt comfortable enough to tell me.

"Your mom is cool with you staying with Nyx? Does she know you got the hots for each other?" I teased, but Dawn's laughter subsided, and a flash of fear replaced her carefree attitude.

Damnit. There I go, ruining it again.

"Sorry, I didn't mean to..."

"No, it's fine. Um, no, I kind of, snuck out." It was my turn to widen my eyes.

"Dawn Price, sneaking out? Say it ain't so!" I feigned shock. She chuckled, but still that light, breezy Dawn that was here just moments ago didn't return.

Guilt clouded over me again.

My mind wandered as I drove to our destination. I had come so close to the same fate once, so close to slipping over the edge. But then, I was saved. At least, it *felt* like I was being saved. Did Dawn have her own angel? Something or someone that had pulled her back? Or had I crossed that line too and just didn't realize it? How would you even know if you were dead? No, I would feel it...*know* it. My angel hadn't let me fall that far. I think.

The more I considered it, the more I doubted that Dawn had a savior like mine. Something else was keeping her here. Unfinished business, maybe? And if I helped her, would I be helping her move on? Sending her to whatever waits on the other side? The thought unsettled me, but I couldn't shake it.

My *savior's* threatening voice echoed in my mind, sending chills down my spine and I found myself thinking that Dawn was better off without him.

"Right here," Dawn's voice pulled me back to reality. I pulled off into the driveway and my eyes scanned the quaint one floor ranch house. The brown siding was decorated for fall with bright colored leaves that we never saw naturally here in Arizona.

"So, what's the plan with all this Sickness stuff?" she asked as her hand rested on the door handle.

I pondered that. I knew I had to do something, but what?

"Something's going to go down at Homecoming tomorrow, and we need to keep as many people away from that drug as possible."

She nodded a few times, absorbing the information. It wasn't much of a plan, or any plan at all really.

"How do we do that?"

Truth be told, I wasn't sure, but it was better than nothing.

"We keep an eye on any shady dealings, or anyone who looks like they're distributing. If Bryce shows up, we watch him like a damn hawk."

She shook her head.

"What if we can't stop them from taking it? What if we can't reach them all?" She urged. I hadn't let myself think that far ahead.

"Then we stop them from succumbing to it." That seemed to placate her.

"I'll make sure I have doses of naloxone on me, just in case." I ran my hands idly along the steering wheel. Dawn eyed me suspiciously. "I got certified to administer a while ago. I didn't have any with me at school that day with Max, I won't be unprepared next time."

"Do we need backup?" She asked, and I found myself ready to blow off her suggested help, but a nagging feeling gripped me in the pit of my stomach. Maybe having help wouldn't be the worst thing in the world. I'd done things alone for so long that it seemed comfortable. Safe. But maybe I didn't have to shoulder this one alone.

"Who are you suggesting?" Her gaze traveled to the front door of the ranch house and I felt a deep sigh escape me.

"They hate me," I whined. Actually whined.

Dawn giggled, climbing out of the junk storm. "Can you blame them?"

No. I couldn't.

I stepped out of the car and followed closely behind, her eyes drifting up to glance at the nearly full moon that hung low above us.

CHAPTER 8

TEAMWORK MAKES MY HEAD ACHE

Nyx was irritable as hell tonight. Maybe even more so than usual. "What the hell are you talking about?" Nyx asked, with their deep throaty accusatory voice. I stifled the impulse to roll my eyes, deciding that I rather liked my arms attached to my body and didn't want to give them any reason to rip them off and swing them around like weapons.

Luckily for me, Dawn stepped in to continue the explanation.

When we arrived at Nyx's ranch house a half hour ago, I was surprised to see not only Nyx and Salem as Dawn said, but also Callum and Nani. The two of them were lounging casually on the couch in the living room, Salem was draped unceremoniously, and yet tantalizingly, across Callum's lap. The two of them were engaged in some serious flirty banter, they didn't even look up from one another as Dawn and I entered the house. Nyx immediately gave me a stare that told me just how welcomed I was in their house, but that animosity washed away the moment a sweet older woman took my hands in hers and smiled at me, leading me in.

"Hello there, sweetheart. You must be Kieran," she cooed.

I cocked an eyebrow towards Nyx, they clearly had been discussing me, it was safe to say it probably wasn't the most flattering.

"Yes ma'am, thank you for letting me crash your party," I said, oozing with the charisma that I usually saved for flirting. "And you must be Nyx's sister?" I heard Nyx scoff as they stalked away, but the woman before me smiled, her wrinkled skin tightening around her bright eyes and she chuckled.

"You are too cute. You hear that Nyx-ie?" She dropped my hand and led me forward into the house, pointing at an array of trays on a dark coffee table. "I made cookies, eat up!" And she scurried away. I smiled after her. I had never even met my own grandparents, not that I wanted to. They kicked my parents out when they came home pregnant, leaving them to fend for themselves. Had they been better parents, maybe I would have had a better chance too. Cycles are a bitch. I reached down to grip a chocolate chip cookie in my hands and felt a pair of eyes on me.

I lifted my head and found Nani's gaze from across the room. I felt my heart rate quicken and my core tightened. The effect this person had on me was starting to be embarrassing. I adjusted myself quickly and took a bite of the cookie to distract my racing heart.

Nani hopped up, and I tried not to rush towards them and beg them to push me against a wall. They made their way over to Dawn, and I sent a quiet plea to my body to behave.

"Casper, took you long enough!" They embraced. My eyes darted to Dawn. That nickname couldn't be a coincidence, could it? Did Nani know? Was Nani also of our particular brand of weird? My mind swirled with questions, but I didn't have time to ask them, because Dawn urged me to spill our secrets, so I launched into action, discussing where we had gone, and what we found. Then after Nyx's angered outburst, Dawn took over, explaining what little we understood.

"So, you t'ink someone is tryin' to kill off an entire student body?" Callum asked, in his thick accent. I tried to ignore Salem's hand that was slowly caressing his thigh, higher, higher....

"Well, it certainly almost killed Max." I answered and saw several faces visibly flinch at that. Right. I probably should have sugar coated that a bit.

"So, what are we supposed to do about it?" Salem asked, sitting up and removing her head from Callum's lap for the first time since I arrived. Her long golden hair hung in loose waves around her face, not a hair out of place despite her human pillow.

Dawn turned to me.

With a sigh, I began describing the loose plan that had been brewing in my head for the past hour.

"We need to keep Bryce from distributing this Sickness at the dance tomorrow. There needs to be eyes on Bryce at all times, and anyone else who could be dealing this shit."

"Like Jace?" Nani chimed in, their accented voice sending a shockwave directly to my groin. I leaned back against the wall, in an attempt to compose myself.

"I don't think Jace is involved in this," I stated matter of factly. Nyx was quick to glare at me.

"Why, because he's your friend and you can't imagine a druggie like him would ever get involved in something like this?" Their eyes glistened with challenge.

"No, because he's a damn idiot who thought The Sickness was a new video game," I threw back, fury lacing my tone. Callum let out a laugh. That seemed to satisfy Nyx for now, they sat back in their recliner and looked over at Dawn who was quietly perched on the arm of the couch.

"So, how do we know who's involved in all this?" Callum asked, and everyone's eyes flashed between myself and Dawn.

"I might be able to find out," Dawn offered in a whisper. I sent her a silent question with my eyes. "I, um, I have pretty good intuition about things. I may be able to get an answer." My mind flashed back to my own shadowed answers that I was able to receive about her. Was she able to look into the nothingness and find truth there too?

"Does anyone know any Sarah's who might be involved?" I asked, glancing around at them.

"I know a Sarah Hawkins who worked at a summer camp with me last year," Salem said. "She's a year younger than us though, and like an honor roll student so I don't know if she'd be involved in this."

My mind flashed to the petite blonde who was in just about every club in school. I've heard her speak at pep rallies, and I was almost positive that voice wasn't hers I heard at Bryce's.

"There's Sarah Gutierrez," Nyx offered. "She's in our grade."

I didn't know her well, had I ever even heard her speak? I wasn't sure.

"I don't know about that," Dawn answered. "I know Sarah a little, her sister Mya, and my brother, Joey, are the same age. She doesn't seem like the druggie type."

I flinched involuntarily.

"I think it would be naive of us to discredit a lead because they 'don't fit the type'," I challenged. "Did Max fit the 'type'?"

Dawn's eyes met mine, and a flash of something crossed her face, like she had just realized what she said and in whose company.

"T'ere's also the possibility it's another college kid Bryce met in class or somethin'?" Callum offered, breaking the tension. I nodded, thankful for the distraction.

"Apparently he has a new roommate from a chemistry lecture," I responded.

"That seems most likely," Nyx chimed in, placing a hand on Dawn's shoulder.

"So, we obviously need to stick together tomorrow, then," Callum said, standing up and clapping his hands together in front of him.

"Wisconsin is right," Nani chimed in, earning a groan from Callum.

"I'm not from Wisconsin!" Callum argued.

"Sure, you're not," Nani said with a wink. I felt my lips curl up in a smile.

"Group date it is." Salem stood. Her mischievous eyes gleamed in the dim light of the couch-side lamp. "I *love* group activities."

I noticed a smile spread across Salem's painted lips, and Dawn and Nyx exchanged a shy glance.

"I kind of, well..." Nyx started, their eyes trained on Dawn. "I kind of already have a date."

Dawn's blush was deep and full, and it warmed my heart to see. Didn't know a ghost could even blush, so there's that. Learning all kinds of new things today.

"Yeah, and I was definitely planning on going stag," Nani responded, their eyes never landing on me. "Nobody's asked me yet."

I smirked, emboldened by that admission.

"Well, I'm asking right now," Salem stated, moving forward and placing a hand on Nani's shoulder. I eyed the spot where their bodies touched, and nearly felt a growl escape my chest. The jealousy spread through my veins like wildfire.

Nani finally looked at me, their dark eyes scanning me

head to toe, undressing me with every flick of their irises. It felt like the room had gotten significantly hotter. Before I realized what I was doing, I had shrugged out of my leather jacket, sporting only my tight blue undershirt. It hugged my biceps tightly, and now with my arms exposed, my tattoos were on full display.

Nani's eyes continued their exploration of my body, as they took their bottom lip in between their teeth.

"Damn, Kieran." Salem's sultry voice drew my gaze from Nani. "You should take your jacket off more often." She let out a low whistle. I smirked at her as she shamelessly scanned me with her eyes.

"So, what'll it be?" Salem said, looking between Callum, Nani and me. "A foursome?" She offered and I couldn't help the image that popped into my head, almost like she planted it there herself. The four of us, writhing beneath each other as we ripped at each other's clothes.

But it wasn't Salem eyes that I couldn't look away from, or Callum's body that had me straining against my jeans. It was Nani.

"I t'ought you were goin' to be all mine tomorrow?" Callum said with feigned disappointment to Salem. Or at least I thought it was feigned.

"I'll make it up to you, I promise," Salem responded, and a dark emotion flashed across Callum's face. He seemed almost upset.

"You should not have said that," Callum warned with a strange edge of seriousness.

Salem, ever the playful one, rocked up on her tiptoes to kiss Callum flat on the mouth. I watched with minimal interest as her mouth devoured Callum's kisses. Their tongues wrestled each other for dominance and their hands began exploring each other's bodies. Callum palmed Salem's ass through her jeans, and Salem's hands disappeared in between their bodies. I could only imagine what she was so eager to get a handful of. It was an erotic and sinful display, and it wasn't helping my already eager state.

"Ahem, you two...seriously?" Nyx called from their spot, Dawn was turned completely away from them.

When they finally pulled away from each other, I saw Salem whisper something into Callum's ear and a dark smirk crossed his face.

"Did I do it?" She asked, fluttering her eyelashes.

"Consider your promise fulfilled." He sounded almost relieved.

"Alright, if that's how our group date is gonna go, Wisconsin, we may never get anything done." Nani smiled as they teased the two. Callum was not hiding his attempt to adjust himself.

"Maybe we need a rule, no funny business 'til we stop Bryce," Callum added, and I think Salem and I pouted at the exact same moment.

"What if they're not going to distribute at the dance?" Nyx said from their spot on the chair. At some point during my wild, inappropriate fantasies, Dawn had moved to perched on the arm of the chair, and Nyx had draped a loose arm around her waist. "What if they wait for the party?"

Shit. Of course. That made perfect sense. Bryce wasn't even a student anymore, if he was going to make a move, the post-homecoming rager was probably going to be the place to do it.

"Right, the one at Ashley Harris' gaff, yes?" Callum answered. My eyes involuntarily flicked over to Dawn. Her face darkened as she pulled her knees to her chest. Nyx seemed unaware of the change.

"Sure, if whatever you just said means house," Nyx answered.

"So, we're going to the party then?" Salem added and I watched Dawn's reactions carefully. The other's nodded, murmuring their agreements, but I held out until Dawn's eyes met mine.

"Yeah, that's a good idea," she responded eventually.

I pitched in my answer, a soft "Okay," and we officially had a plan.

"What do we do if we can't stop them from distributing?" Salem offered as she slid back down onto the couch.

"I'm naloxone certified, and I have a few emergency doses." Everyone's eyes landed on me and my face heated under their pitying gazes. They were empathetic, even Nyx's eyes softened as they analyzed the 'poor little drug boy'.

"But it's not a lot, it will only help a few people," I added quickly.

Nani took a few bounding steps across the living room and stopped in front of me. "I have an old family recipe, a bit of a home remedy. If the situation calls for it." Their face screwed up with disgust at the thought of whatever this 'remedy' was. I was about to ask something but their hand landed on my bare forearm and the electricity that shot through my body stopped my thoughts dead in their tracks.

Their dark brown hair was pulled back into a bun at the nape of their neck, and their bronze skin looked sinful against my inked arms. I watched their fingers as they delicately traced the design on my forearm with their thumb.

"Someone tell me why we aren't just going to the cops with this information?" Nyx asked in the silent living room. Nani's hand ceased moving, but they did not break the contact.

"Because I don't want Max to get in trouble." Dawn stated, quietly.

"Plus, something tells me, whatever is going on here is beyond the authorities capabilities." I didn't need to elaborate, Dawn understood, and it seemed as if everyone was willing to accept my word on it.

"How is he, by the way," I asked. "Max. Is he alright?"

Dawn and Callum shared a look, being the two who were the closest to him.

"He's recoverin'," Callum said. "But it's been a rough road. His parents are convinced he would never take any drugs, so they're fussing over him t'inking something else must be going on."

I nodded my head. "I'm glad he's okay." And damn, I meant it. I'd seen my fair share of drug-related tragedies and I did not want to add Max to the exclusive list of deaths I've witnessed.

"So, we have a plan," Callum said, glancing around at each of us. His golden eyes met mine with a strange desperation.

"And we have a backup," I added.

"Let's stop this Sickness," Dawn finished, her voice hard and serious.

The clock read nearly midnight, I thanked Nyx for their hospitality, which was met with a shrug and a nod - progress, I'd take it - and eased out the front door into the cool Arizona night air.

I loved the sky at night, when the stars had nowhere to hide. Sometimes I wished I hadn't found my own hiding spots. The places I disappeared to in order to be alone. So much of my existence was spent crawling from shadow to shadow, remaining hidden. I didn't want to let myself think about what life would be like if things were different. If I didn't have to be alone. If I didn't have to hide in the shadows.

But that's not possible. I wasn't meant to be in the light. I was meant to be alone.

"Yo, Special K, slow down."

My heart tightened at the voice calling me from behind. I contained a sigh, and turned to face Nani Ka'ana, as they bounded down the driveway toward me.

"Special K?" I asked, lifting an eyebrow as they approached.

"Thought it fit." They smiled, placing their hands on their hips. I held my jacket in my hand, and felt the cool night air hit my exposed skin, which was ice cold compared to the heat I felt in their presence.

"I like it," I said truthfully, letting my smile widen.

"So, you gonna give me a ride home or what?"

I glanced back at the house, nobody else seemed to be leaving.

"Who'd you ride with?"

"Salem and Nyx, but they're staying the night here." They mindlessly ran their tongue along their bottom lip, and I damn near leaned forward to taste it.

"You weren't invited to the sleepover either?" I joked, and they laughed, the sound hitting me directly at my core, fanning the already growing fire.

"Oh, I was," Nani said, glancing back at the house over their shoulder. My eyes couldn't help but follow the move-ment, trailing down to their neck. The way the muscles stretched and tensed as they turned made me wonder how their neck would look if I had my fingers tangled in their hair, pulling just enough to tilt their head back.

"But I'd much rather spend the night with you."

My eyebrows shot up in surprise and a startled chuckle escaped my mouth at their admission.

"So, you want me to take you home?" I confirmed, and

they nodded slowly, their eyes trailing my chest. "And that's all?"

"A lot can happen in a ten minute drive," they taunted, and I felt my core tighten with excitement.

"Well, allow me to lead the way." I turned toward my car, tossing the slightest look over my shoulder to ensure they were following me.

Sliding into the driver's seat, I barely had a chance to breathe before Nani settled beside me, shutting out the world with the sound of the door closing. Then their lips were on mine. The kiss was hungry, a clash of warmth and want as their mouth claimed mine. Their tongue traced the seam of my lips, coaxing them open, and I gave in without hesitation. When their tongue pressed into my mouth, my fingers found their way to their hair, tangling in the soft strands as I pulled them closer to me, desperate to erase the space the center console stubbornly maintained between us.

Their fingers clung into the collar of the shirt and pulled me into them, their lips drinking from mine as if they had been deprived of life's sweetest delicacies and I was a bar of chocolate. The car filled with a steamy symphony of moans and delicious sounds of our wet mouths taking what they needed from each other. Nani pulled at my hair, and I let out a deep throaty groan as the movement sent me tumbling mind-lessly into a completely frenzied state. Their lips returned to my skin at the base of my neck. Their wet tongue licking a trail up to the base of my jaw and moving with a devious need to my earlobe.

"I haven't been able to stop thinking about you," they whispered into my ear, their warm breath sending shivers down my spine, my fingers dug into their hips. "About all the things I've wanted to do to you." A whimper escaped my throat at the sinful promise on their lips.

Their mouth met mine again and this time Nani took their time exploring the expanse of my kiss with their skilled tongue.

"Fuck, Nani," I cried into their mouth. I felt their lips upturn into a wicked smirk against our kiss.

"I intend to." Nani's hand dove down to my lap, landing on the painful bulge of my length. The gentle touch nearly sent me tumbling into an early finish, and I silently begged that I could prolong this moment forever.

Nani's lips brushed softly down my neck, trailing along the edge of my shirt collar. I leaned back in my seat, breath coming in shallow pants as my eyes darted to the empty street outside. A single streetlamp cast its dim, orange glow over the pavement, but the surrounding shadows cloaked us in privacy. For now, at least.

"I need to taste you, Kieran." Holy shit.

I pushed my hands into their hair and pulled their mouth to mine again.

"Ah, ah, ah..." they taunted, pulling away. "Did you forget who is in charge here?" My breath caught in my throat as Nani slowly unbuttoned my jeans. I felt my heart might actually burst through my chest if I didn't get their mouth on me immediately.

They made quick work of releasing my length from its fabric prison. It sprung to life, looking eagerly stretched and waiting. Nani's eyes surveyed me hungrily, their mouth hovering inches from my skin.

"You've missed me, haven't you?" they whispered, their breath hitting the tip of my length and sending a jolt of desire directly to my core.

"God, yes." I wasn't sure I was even making any sense anymore, but it didn't matter. I needed Nani's mouth and I needed it now. "Nani." Our eyes met in the darkness of the car, their skin looked like smooth silk in the dim glow of the street lamps.

"Beg for it."

Nani's mouth inched closer until I felt the phantom brush of their lips against the spot that was desperate for them. Their fingers danced along my thighs, moving ever closer to my center.

"I need you. Now. Please." I nearly screamed, all common sense had left me.

"I can't hear you, Kieran." Their tongue darted out, stopping just short of making contact.

"Nani! Please. Fuck!" Their tongue met my skin and a delicious hiss escaped at the feeling. A jolt of pleasure shot through me as they swirled their wet tongue around the head, just the way I needed them to. "Yes...God." I felt Nani's chest shake with laughter, but the only sound that escaped was the sinful wetness as they closed their mouth around me and took me deep into their throat. I saw fucking stars. They opened their throat for me, taking me entirely to the base. The sound that echoed in the car almost had me catapulting off the edge already. But I wasn't ready to be done with them. I don't think I ever would be.

Their head bobbed up and down, working me like it was their only purpose. Their tongue flicked the sensitive skin at the tip, and I found myself reaching for their hair again, but stopped just short. Restraining myself. Forcing myself to behave.

Their fingers gently swept against my lower abs, which were tightly clenched. I cried out as the euphoric feeling gripped me. They continued to work me, delivering a pleasure I only ever found with them, and periodically dancing along my stomach with their fingers until my entire body shivered.

I was a goner. I felt myself topple over the edge of oblivion, my muscles contracting over and over as stars clouded my vision. Nani remained still, only removing their lips from my throbbing length when they were sure they had wrung every ounce of pleasure from my body.

My moans turned to deep sighs as I struggled to maintain my breathing. I was pretty sure my pounding heart could be heard from miles away.

Nani sat up, licking their lips, and smiled at me. I reached for their face, and pulled them down to me. I kissed them with everything I had left. The taste of my salty release still echoed on their tongue.

"Well, see you soon Special K," Nani spoke abruptly, gripping the door handle.

"Wait, what?" I asked, shocked. " I thought I was taking you home." My breathing still hadn't returned to normal.

"You think I'd pass up a sleepover with Casper, Salem, Wisconsin, and Nyx? Yeah right."

I tried not to let it show how jealous I was that I wasn't the only one that garnered a nickname, but the only one who didn't garner an invite. They hopped from the car, but leaned down to say one last thing. "You taste even better than I remember."

I watched them, dumbfoundedly, as they climbed the driveway back to the house. I tucked myself away and refastened my jeans, forcing myself to breathe. Pulling from the driveway I crept slowly through the neighborhood, my headlights the only source of light in the darkness of the desert.

You chose them again...

My Angel's voice dripped with desperation and anger.

Are you ready to fulfill your promise to me?

I couldn't help the shudder that ran through my body as I nodded.

Bring me Salem Bridges.

My heart rate spiked.

"Why do you need Salem? She seems fine?" She was well-adjusted, confident, she had friends...

Ask me another fucking question and see what happens, boy!

The voice roared, a chaotic symphony of malice and anger that reverberated through my skull. I clutched my temple as the searing pain drove into my mind like a dagger.

"I'm...I'm confused," I whispered, painfully, pleading with the voice in my head.

You chose to be with a soulless creature, now you owe me someone of my choosing. Those were the terms.

Something was different about the voice now, I couldn't quite put my finger on it. It sounded... more guttural, as if the facade of angelic grace was starting to crack, exposing something far more dangerous beneath. Fear crept through my veins, cold and steady.

"And you want to help them..." I whispered, my voice betraying my fear.

You don't believe me? It taunted in a sinister whisper.

I shook my head. "I don't understand."

Our arrangement is simple, Kieran. I saved your pathetic little life, and in return, you bring me tortured souls.

I gasped, gripping the steering wheel. "I thought you were saving them."

I am.

"I want to be with Nani," I said carefully, turning toward my side of town. It wasn't something I planned to admit, but I was surprised to see just how truthful it felt. I did. I wanted to be with them. They made me feel like myself, like I didn't have to be alone or hide any more.

Are you under the impression that I care what you want?

I jolted. This angel, the one who had saved me from the brink of nothingness, who had introduced me to the abyss and taught me that I could be so much more than the drug addict I had become, was far less heavenly than I had believed.

"I thought you did," I stuttered.

The voice chuckled darkly, echoing in my skull. My fingers were tense and sore from just how tightly I was gripping the wheel.

Kieran, you have become bold. Too bold. I think it might be time for you to be reminded why you're still alive.

Just as I opened my mouth to ask what he meant, something inside me snapped. It was as if the very polarity of my moral compass had shifted, flipping everything I thought I knew upside down. Suddenly, the only truth that mattered was the one my Angel spoke. All the doubt and fear that had weighed on me vanished, replaced by a rush of honor and devotion. I had been foolish, careless, and ungrateful.

I was wasting the life I didn't deserve, the gift my Angel had given me. And that realization brought a sharp sting of shame.

Do you understand now, Kieran? My Angel's voice was steady, almost gentle.

"Of course," I whispered, my throat tight with disgust at my own behavior. I was going to make things right. I would atone for my mistakes, prove my worth to the one who had saved me. My Angel had given me life. My Angel had given me purpose. And my Angel did not deserve to be questioned.

My Angel required souls...and I would bring them to him.

Good. Now, go get me Salem.

CHAPTER 9

COUNTDOWN TO FREEDOM

HOMECOMING WAS a night of frivolity and debauchery where even the most buttoned up of people found themselves letting loose and making decisions their parents would be shocked by. It brought with it an air of confidence, risk-taking and the love of being young. A perfect cocktail for finding lost and tortured souls who needed saving. I spent most of the day preparing for the evening to come. I donned a white button down, leaving the top three buttons undone and rolling the sleeves up to my elbows, and pairing it with tight red dress pants that left little to the imagination. I knew that I had some groveling to do tonight for my Angel, and I needed to utilize every weapon in my arsenal.

I stared at the naloxone sitting on my counter. I had promised to bring it in case this Sickness made its way through the student body tonight. But the Kieran that was worried about all of that seemed buried so deep now that I almost left without pocketing them.

Call it curiosity, or defiance, but I found myself slipping back into my kitchen to grab the doses just before getting into my car to head to the dance. Remembering that my Angel also wanted me to stop whatever Bryce had planned.

Bring me Salem, and four others tonight as penance, Kieran. Then I will forgive you.

Hope bloomed in my chest. I hated feeling like I had disappointed the only person who ever truly cared about me. I needed his forgiveness like I needed air.

The streets were alive with energy as I approached the school. My classmates milled about excitedly as they ventured inside, their bodies draped in colorful, sparkly, and tailored attire. My eyes scanned the crowd eagerly, looking at each face and seeing them differently now. They weren't my classmates, they were souls who needed protecting. Souls that needed to be introduced to my Angel.

I needed five of them to prove to my Angel that I deserved his love. I was eager to get started. Once I was parked, I slid out of the car and slowly surveyed the surrounding area. The blur of excited faces were intoxicating, their joy infectious. I didn't need joy though, I needed despair, fear, anger.

One kiss should do it.

His voice promised. I knew that intimacy was a way to bring my Angel closer to others. It had worked with Brett, after all. The part of me that had been hurt by Brett just a few days ago stirred briefly, but I smothered it down, locking it away. There were souls to be claimed, and that was my focus now.

I began the slow walk toward the front door when a voice called out to me. "Looking good, Andras."

I turned toward the source of the sound, a smile tugging at my lips when I saw Rhonda and Emma walking toward me. They both wore strapless dresses that hugged their figures, Rhonda in a deep emerald green and Emma in a soft purple. I tilted my head as I took them in. Emma seemed uneasy, her shyness practically radiating, while Rhonda, as usual, exuded her typical attention-seeking energy.

They will do.

I licked my lips.

"Ladies," I cooed, stepping toward them. "You both look..." a low whistle escaped my lips as I scanned their outfits with a lingering gaze. "You look great."

Rhonda preened at the compliment, and Emma blushed softly.

"Who are the lucky people who get to call you dates tonight?" I asked. Not that the presence of a date would keep me from my goal, but I'd like to know who's fists were going to come flying when I earned my kisses from them.

"We're going together," Emma responded quickly. Her eyes darted to the ground, but I could see the heat creeping into her cheeks.

"So, we can dance with everybody," Rhonda added quickly.

I nodded, licking my bottom lip again and watching as the two of them tracked the movement. I leaned in, my face between theirs and I heard both of them inhale sharply.

"Lucky me," I whispered, lingering between the two of them. I turned my head only slightly toward Rhonda, giving her the most seductive look I could muster and she took it for the invitation that it was. Pressing her painted lips against mine. She kissed like someone who was starving for affection and desperate for attention. I gave her both and somehow I felt lighter. As if the weight of my Angel's disappointment had shrunk with each swipe of her tongue against mine. I pulled my face back, just enough to smile at Rhonda and then turned to see Emma. Her face was red, and she was breathing shallowly. Her bare lips were parted as she studied me.

"You didn't wear any lipstick today," I noted, leaning toward her again. She gulped, shaking her head.

"I think this color would look great on you," I tease, indicating the smear of Rhonda's makeup on my lips.

She nodded, and I leaned in, taking her lips with mine. She kissed like she was afraid of being bad at it. So I slid an arm around her waist and felt her body relax against mine. Her timid kiss was fine, nothing transcendent or passionate, but I smiled against her lips as I felt my Angel grab hold of her through me.

I pulled back, beaming at the two of them, feeling wickedly similar to a marionette who was suddenly two cut strings closer to freedom.

"Ladies, you spoil me. I haven't even made it inside yet and I feel like I've been crowned King." They giggled at my compliment as I pulled my arm away from the two of them. "I'll see you in there. Try to save a dance for me," I teased with a wink. Rhonda tried to lean in for another kiss, but I took a few steps away. The disappointment flashed on her face for only a moment before she linked her arm with Emma's and the two of them rushed inside.

When they were out of my line of sight, my charming smile dropped, as I ran the back of my palm across my mouth to remove the remnants of my kiss with Rhonda.

That's two, Kieran. Good boy.

I preened at the praise and fixed a smirk on my face before sauntering in.

'Who else do you want?' I asked silently as I entered the lobby of the school and was met with a sea of eager teenagers. Faces I knew, faces I didn't. Faces I wish I never had to see again.

Brett was easy to pick out of the crowd. With his perfect fucking skin, and expertly tailored suit. His garish excuse for a girlfriend fawning over him in a dress that should never have been made. I felt anger simmer through my blood as I surveyed her.

Good choice.

For a brief moment, shock flooded my emotions, but I kept my mouth shut. I'd learned better than to ask questions. Instead, I moved forward, positioning myself just within her line of sight. Once I felt her eyes on me, I let my gaze slowly trace her body, making sure to hide the disdain I felt. I must've played it well because she blushed, and when our eyes met again, I noticed the heat there. I dragged my tongue across my lips, watching as her eyes followed the movement, her focus intense. Then, I bit my bottom lip. She practically melted under my attention. I let my stare linger a little longer before slipping into the gym, knowing she'd come to find me when she was ready.

Until then, I still need one more...

And then I needed Salem.

The gymnasium was alive with bass heavy music and flashing colorful lights that danced along the floor and the walls. Bodies writhed against each other seductively to the beat. The bleachers had been opened so that students could sit atop them... or disappear beneath them. My eyes scanned the crowd, waiting for the signal that I had another choice for my Angel.

My eyes paused on a pair sitting alone on the bleachers. Nyx and Dawn. I would finish what my angel needed, then we could focus on the plan. But just as I aimed to pull my eyes from them...

Dawn.

The Angel whispered.

I frowned, hesitation clawing at me. I didn't like this decision, but I'd already made enough mistakes to add one more to the pile. I had to prove I was worth saving, and if being with Dawn Price was what it took, then that's what I'd do. I made my way toward the bleachers, my eyes fixed on the pale, quiet girl no one realized was dead. As I approached, her gaze lifted to meet mine, a hint of confusion flickering across her face. Just as I was about to step onto the bottom row of bleachers, a hand gripped my arm, halting me. I turned to find Ashley standing there, her eyes burning as she stared at me.

"Ashley," I said, infusing as much charm as I could muster.

"Kieran," she replied, coyly, batting her eyelashes at me. I let my eyes wander the length of her body again, ensuring to stop long enough at her cleavage for her to notice.

"You look...edible," I whispered, relishing the way her cheeks burned red under my gaze.

"You can't keep looking at me like that," she said in a way that told me there was no actual truth in her statement.

"And why not?" I asked, leaning in invitingly.

She closed the gap, bringing her lips to my ear and whispered, "Because my boyfriend will get jealous."

I resisted the urge to tell her that she had no idea how true that statement was.

"I don't care," I said, pressing my lips against her ear, letting my breath dance across her skin. She moaned slightly.

"Wait for me under the bleachers. I'll be there in two minutes," she said, pulling back to meet my gaze. I couldn't help but notice the way her chest rose and fell, her pupils dark and wide. She wanted me, and part of me was torn between satisfying my Angel's desires and rubbing it in my ex's face.

She walked off, and I watched her for a moment before my gaze shifted back to the two of them on the bleachers. But I wasn't ready for the punch to the gut that came with the look on Dawn's face. Betrayal, hurt, anger, every emotion she felt was aimed squarely at me, and it hit harder than I expected.

At that moment, I wanted nothing more than to explain myself to her, to tell her why I needed to do this, but the tight grip my Angel still had on me kept those words locked inside. Instead of confronting the tension between us, I turned away and made my way under the bleachers, leaving everything unsaid.

It turned out Ashley wasn't the only person intending on meeting up under the bleachers because I saw two other couples going at it on my way to a secluded section. There I waited in the dark, my heart pumping blood at a furious rate. I was so close to being forgiven, so close to fulfilling my promise. So close to making my Angel proud.

"There you are," Ashley's voice pulled me back to reality and I turned to see her approach me.

"Here I am," I replied, oozing with the sexual charm I knew expected from me.

"I've wanted to try a bad boy for a long time, Kieran," she whispered, pushing up against me, her breasts pressed into my chest as her hands danced along my arms.

"Are you sure you're up for it?" I teased, slowly raising the skirt of her dress. Her fingers popped open the button of my dress pants and she nimbly pulled my length from its place. I held the excess fabric of her skirt pooled around her waist, exposing her core to me. She lined me up with her slick opening.

"Show me how you do it on the wrong side of the tracks," she demanded before slamming down onto me. Another string holding me in my place of punishment snapped as she rode me, her face twisted in pleasure. I pulled her close to me, just so I could bury her face in the crook of my neck and avoid looking at her.

Then I saw him. Quietly standing in the dark shadows of the bleachers. His eyes locked onto mine. He didn't make a move to interrupt. And he didn't even look all that mad. Instead, his eyes burned with a different emotion.

Lust.

I slammed into Ashley harder, suddenly feeling the need to perform for my audience. She whimpered in my hold.

"Say my name," I commanded her. She moaned against my neck. "Say it."

"Kieran," she cried out as her climax found her. She shuttered in my embrace and I let her body tremble as I stared at him.

I lifted her off of me, and she whimpered.

"You didn't finish," she pouted, looking down at my still erect length.

"I wasn't the important one," I replied, pretending it had everything to do with me wanting her pleasure and her pleasure alone and not my lack of desire to keep touching her for a single second more.

"You're just as good as I thought you'd be," she complimented, pressing her lips against my throat again. "Hopefully, this isn't the last time."

"You head out first," I replied, not justifying her thirst with a response. She smiled, eyes clouded and cheeks red and she turned to leave. My eyes found him again. She didn't see him, she never saw him, not like I did.

He stepped forward, his eyes flicking down toward my erection which I hadn't covered up.

"Did you enjoy the show, Brett?" I asked him, quietly. My gaze burned into his.

"Did you fuck her to piss me off?" He seethed.

"Did it work?"

He took another step closer, his chest nearly pressing against mine now.

"Fuck you, Kieran," he spat, his eyes burning with anger, regret and most of all desire.

"Did you like watching me make her tremble?" I tease, my voice unnaturally grim. "Did you see how she called my name? Has she ever screamed your name like that?"

"Shut up," he growled.

"Tell me, Brett. When you were watching us, did you wish you were me...or her?"

His fist flew quickly, slamming into my cheek. The rush of pain was vicious but worth it to see the look on his face.

I already have his soul in my hands. My Angel whispered into my mind. *But if you give me more of him, maybe I can make him mine. Just like you.*

'You want more of him?' I asked.

I want all of him.

I let the command wash over me. Unthinking and resolved to finally prove to my Angel that I was worth his love and his attention. I felt almost numb to his command.

"Do you want me, Brett?" I asked, anger and fury lacing my tone.

"Fuck you," he said again, but the way his breath hitched and his eyes flicked toward my length again, I knew he did.

"Then get on your fucking knees, and take me." I braced myself for another punch, and by the way his fists clenched at his sides, he very nearly did. But then, he sank to his knees and with fury in his gaze, he took me into his mouth.

My head fell back as he worked his mouth over my sensitive, aching length.

"Make me come, and I'll forgive you for watching me fuck your girlfriend." It was a potentially dangerous game to play as he had his teeth so close to my most delicate parts, but I knew his turn ons, and anger was one of them. He growled around my length, the vibrations sending me toppling over the edge into a climax.

Before I could even calm my breathing, he stood, wrapped his hands around my throat and pushed me back against the brace of the bleachers. I did not allow fear to show on my face, but I certainly felt an inkling of it for a moment as I took in the pure loathing in his eyes when he looked at me.

"I hate you, Kieran Andras," Brett spat, his lips brushing against mine as he put pressure onto my windpipe.

"I know," I replied softly with what little air he was allowing me. His lips hovered over mine in a torturously tempting distance. His chest was heaving, wild unrestrained anger just below the surface. His eyes softened, but his hold on my throat did not.

"But I think I fucking love you."

Was I shocked that he felt that way? Not at all. After the summer of passion we had, I think even the most repressed people would begin to feel something. Hell, there was a time I thought maybe I felt that way, too. But was I shocked that he admitted it? Abso-fucking-lutely.

"I know," I replied just before he pressed his punishing lips against mine. I did not kiss him back as his hungry lips sought comfort with mine. He kissed me like a man who was broken, a man who was lost. A man who had nothing left to lose.

But I wasn't broken because my Angel fixed me.

I wasn't lost because my Angel found me.

And I had everything to lose.

"Votes are in and this year's homecoming queen is Ashley Harris!" Cheers erupted in the gymnasium, but Brett continued to ravage my mouth with his. His tongue sweeping through the seam of my mouth to claim me as his.

His kisses were desperate, determined.

And yet, I didn't want them.

The part of me that could have loved Brett Jacobs had long disappeared, and now only primal lust and deep disgust-filled loathing remained.

This kiss wasn't for me.

This kiss was for my Angel.

"And your homecoming King, Brett Jacobs!" He pulled away, panting as the sound of the roaring crowd echoed. He stumbled back, finally releasing my throat from his grasp. I sucked in a lungful of air.

"Better run along," I whispered, fastening my pants. He adjusted himself, as best he could, but I knew everyone would be able to recognize the disheveled appearance and the flushed skin tone. I took pride in the fact that they would know. That they would be able to tell that someone had made him come undone.

Someone had ruined him.

"Brett! Where are you at?" the announcer called again.

"We need to talk about this," he said.

"We already have," I replied. "Get out of my sight."

He looked torn, broken, but instead of fighting me he sauntered off leaving me alone once again.

Your dedication to me is not unnoticed, Kieran.

'Thank you,' I whispered back to him.

Just get me Salem, and forgiveness is yours.

'Will a kiss do?' I asked. Knowing that I'd be willing to go the extra mile for my Angel, but feeling suddenly drained.

For now, yes.

One more kiss, and then I'm back in his good graces. That hope bloomed in my chest, easing some of the anxious nerves that have been so prevalent since I had betrayed him.

I stepped out from under the bleachers just in time to see Brett and Ashley venturing onto the dance floor to have their dance as King and Queen. Her makeup was smeared, her hair disheveled, his shirt untucked, face flushed and his eyes were dilated. The whole gym might have believed it was each other that they fell apart with. But they both knew the truth.

And so did I.

And so did my Angel.

I diverted my eyes from the picture perfect couple at the center of the room and climbed the bleachers toward where Dawn and Nyx had been. As luck would have it, Salem and Callum had arrived as well and found a seat near the others. There was no sign of Nani yet, but that was a fact I was thankful for. My Angel doesn't like being near them. As I approached, Salem flashed a bright and inviting smile in my direction. I plastered a charming smirk on my lips and beelined directly for her. Her golden hair was curled loosely, hanging in large ringlets across her bare shoulders. Her dark red dress matched my dress pants nearly perfectly.

"About time you showed up," Nyx said as I reached them. My eyes flicked away from Salem for a moment to acknowledge them.

"Had some things to take care of," I offered with a shrug.

"Was one of those things Ashley Harris?" Nyx chided, and this time when I looked toward them, I saw Dawn's meek form beside them, nearly folding in on herself.

I knew then that something was wrong with me, because I should have felt shame. I should have felt guilt for what I'd done after what Dawn revealed to me last night. But where that morality normally lies, was nothing but numbness.

You've no use for petty emotions, boy.

I wanted to apologize, I think. I wanted to fight back. But all I could think was how close I was to fulfilling my promise to my Angel.

"She wishes," I said with a wink. "So does her boyfriend."

Nyx shot me an annoyed look before turning to whisper

something to Dawn. She nodded shyly, avoiding eye contact with me before offering a reply to them. A hand on my arm drew my attention back to Salem. Her freshly manicured nails danced delicately on my exposed forearm, tracing along the lines of the tattoos there.

"You look great, Kieran," she said seductively.

"I look even better up close," I challenged with a raised eyebrow.

"I disagree," Callum stated matter of factly from his seat. His accent exaggerated. I ignored him and smiled back at the bombshell before me.

"So, what's a boy gotta do to get a kiss hello?" I teased and watched as her eyes darkened with lust.

"Don't tempt me with a good time," she tossed back smiling.

I plopped down onto the bleachers, taking a seat beside her. "We match," I said, brushing my thigh against hers and indicating the similar shades.

"You're very flirty tonight," she replied, placing a hand on my knee.

"Isn't that what homecoming is all about? Letting loose and flirting with pretty people?" I said, leaning toward her so that our breath mingled.

"Not when there's a drug going around that might kill some people," Nyx replied, gruffly.

"We've already agreed to a group date," Callum interjected, throwing his arm around Salem's shoulders. "And no funny business remember!" He used his hand to push against my shoulder, trying to put distance between Salem and I.

"Well, I could try to focus, but it'll be hard," I said, exaggerating my disappointment and letting my thigh press harder against hers.

"What can I do to help you focus?" Salem asked, leaning her body into mine.

"I'm gonna barf," Nyx whispered, followed by a faux gagging sound.

I caught Salem's sultry eyes with mine, nearly closed the space between us and then whispered darkly, "Kiss me." My eyes flicked to her lips for a moment then back to her gaze just as she made the decision. She pressed her painted lips against mine, softly. There was a quiet sort of lust behind it, nothing hungry or desperate.

Suddenly, the clouds that had dulled my mind broke apart, the numbness giving way to the torrent of guilt and shame I had been bracing myself to feel. It poured in, raw and sharp, filling every part of me until it ached. I could barely breathe as the weight of what my Angel had asked of me, of what I had done so blindly and recklessly, crashed down around me. I hadn't questioned it. I hadn't thought twice. And now, with my breath tight and shallow, the realization pressed on me.

My Angel was not my savior. He was my downfall.

Salem's lips continued to press against mine, warm and steady, offering a comfort that felt both grounding and dangerous. I surrendered to the kiss, letting its softness wash over me, if only to drown out the reckoning that waited on the other side.

Salem's kiss deepened, and I sank further, feeling the warmth fade, replaced by something strange, a pulling sensation, almost like a quiet siphon. It was subtle at first, like the gentle tug of an undertow, but then it intensified. My limbs felt heavier, my chest hollow, as though something essential was slipping away. I tried to pull back, but Salem held me closer, her fingers threading through my hair, keeping me anchored to her. My heartbeat faltered, each beat slower than the last, and a cold numbness crept into my skin, as if she were absorbing the very essence of me with every second that passed.

Stop! Stop now!

His voice echoed in my head and I pulled back from Salem. She smiled at me sweetly, unaware of the command I had just followed or the hollowness in my soul. My chest ached, whether from the weight of my senses returning, or the feeling of being drained, I wasn't sure, but I knew I needed to find a moment to compose myself.

I stood quickly.

"I need to use the restroom," I uttered, shell shocked, monotone.

"Ugh, Jesus, Kieran. You can't wait till you get home to... deal with that?" Nyx argued, making a disgusted face. For the first time, I agreed with their disdain for me.

"Ha ha, very funny, Nyx. No, I seriously just need to go," I replied, trying to feign normalcy despite the tumultuous storm brewing beneath my skin. "Thanks for the wake up call, gorgeous," I tossed over my shoulder at Salem who had sunk back into Callum's hold.

I tried to catch Dawn's eyes, but she was still avoiding my gaze. For fucking good reason. I don't know if she believed the lie I gave, but I hoped she did.

I'd make it up to her when I could. If I could. But right now, I needed to be free from this room and the crushing weight of this detox.

I hurried down the bleachers, brushing past the other students with little regard. The beat of the music pounded in my skull, each throb syncing with the ache twisting through me. The crowd blurred into swirls of eager faces and pulsating lights, the sounds more like static in my ears. I stumbled forward, barely aware of the arms brushing against me, eyes flashing with concern or curiosity as I pushed past them. My hands shook, my skin was damp with sweat and something else. Something that felt dirty, poisoned.

I just needed to get out. To be alone. The edges of the room seemed to threaten to collapse inward as I stumbled toward the locker room, my breath coming in shallow gasps, fighting the nausea that was growing in my chest. This feeling, this crawling sensation under my skin, was too familiar, like a bitter memory resurfacing. The walls of the locker room felt too close, the fluorescent lights harsh and unflinching, exposing every crack in the armor I'd built in the past year.

My legs gave out, and I slumped forward, gripping the sides of the sink to steady myself. My eyes caught my reflection in the dirty mirror before me, and I didn't recognize the man I saw. I was crashing, coming down hard. Like a detox, but worse. There was this hollow ache that pulsed from the center of me, the truth behind this withdrawal stabbing through the haze.

This "angel" was never going to save me. He was an addiction that would kill me.

This entity that I'd trusted blindly, had twisted my mind, my actions, made me into something I didn't recognize. It had taken me over, steering me with promises and whispers, and I had let it. Bile rose in my throat as I stared at my reflection. Ashamed of the person who looked back.

You're regretting your choice. The voice said, low, threateningly.

"What just happened?" I asked out loud, my voice was strained and weak.

It appears your acquaintance has a powerful bond of her very own.

My brow furrowed.

"What do you mean?"

She was draining our power. He responded, anger laced in his tone. *Little Salem has a devil on her side.*

My heart skipped a beat.

"A devil?" I whispered. "What does that mean?"

It means that things just got a little more complicated for us, Kieran.

"What are you planning to do with the souls I bring you?" I asked, meeting my eyes in the mirror, my knuckles going white from the grip I held on the edge of the sink.

Tsk. Tsk. Tsk. His voice sent shivers down my spine. I felt him everywhere, echoing in my mind. *I thought you had learned your lesson by now, little boy.*

As his wicked voice filled my mind, berating me with its harsh, biting words, I looked into the mirror and saw my own face begin to twist, like it was being molded by someone else's hands. My reflection split, fractured almost perfectly down the center, one half still me, but the other half...something else entirely. A figure of black, swirling smoke took over, dark and ominous, as though it were bleeding into my skin. Its eyes glowed a dark, hellish red, piercing through me, and its mouth was stretched in a wicked, unnatural smile that curved nearly to the earlobe, a grin of twisted pleasure.. The longer I looked, the harder it was to distinguish where my face ended and its began. I wanted to look away, but I couldn't. I was trapped in the intensity of those burning eyes, feeling both fear and a strange, warped sense of imprisonment as its presence wrapped around me, as if reminding me that I belonged to it... and that I would never be free.

Have you forgotten so easily? Have you forgotten that you owe me your life? That I am your savior?

I tried to push his voice away, to brace against the onslaught of his fury, but I felt weak against his hold.

Do you think you deserve anything other than the life of a submissive? The life of MY submissive?

I cringed, feeling the piercing dagger of his words ripped into my chest.

You have no right to ask anything of me, Kieran. Have I made myself perfectly clear?

I watched the reflection, the eager and wicked face staring back at me from the once familiar canvas of my own.

I tried to shake my head, to disagree, but deep down in the darkened shadows of my soul, I knew that he was speaking the truth. I should be dead.

I was dead...

You have a task, Kieran. Stop this Sickness. They are interfering with my plans.

"They?" I asked, but suddenly it was quiet. The pressure of his presence had dissipated and for the first time in over a day, I was alone. I let my fingers dance along my face, now returned to normal, but the phantom feeling of his smokey skin felt too real, too all-consuming.

I felt hollow, weak. He who had once made me feel so full of hope and purpose had left me feeling empty and aimless.

And for the first time since my overdose, I craved a high.

CHAPTER 10

IT'S LIKE CARRIE, BUT WORSE

SLIPPING out of the locker room and back into the gymnasium was nearly impossible. My body felt heavy and I could feel the weight of my actions sink into me. My thoughts drifted to the five people I'd delivered to my "angel," no questions asked. What would come of them? What were the consequences of my recklessness going to be?

The music had picked back up after the royal slow dance between Ashley and Brett, a match made in hell honestly, and the dance floor was packed with writhing, sweaty bodies chasing their pleasure with partners to the beat of some top 40 hits.

I shamefully climbed the bleachers toward the group I'd somehow fallen in line with and felt their stares as I approached.

"You good?" Nyx asked, with maybe a twinge of concern.

"You worried about me Nyx-ie?" I teased, trying to regain a modicum of composure. They scoffed and rolled their eyes, which ironically made me feel quite normal for a moment.

"Special K, you clean up nice," Nani, who had finally joined us, said, drawing my gaze to them. They wore a button down, barely buttoned, and tight dark pants hugging their muscular thighs. I let my gaze appreciate them for a moment longer than was probably considered 'polite.'

"Thanks," I responded before meeting their eyes again. God, the things I would do for them. Concerning, dangerous things. But then a shock of guilt slammed into me again for thinking of my own pleasure in a time like this.

"Alright then, what's the plan?" Callum said, drawing my attention from Nani. "How do we stop the Sickness?"

I glanced out over the sea of our classmates, scanning the area for anything that might seem out of place, but ultimately found nothing.

"I think it's going to happen at the after-party, like you said," I confirmed.

"Can we just go around telling everyone not to take the drug?" Nyx offered matter-of-factly.

"Yeah, go tell a bunch of horny, drunk, rebellious teenagers NOT to do something. I've seen that work out real well in the past," I tossed back, not with ire, but a healthy dose of sarcasm.

"Well, what do you suggest we do then?" Nyx clapped back.

I turned to face them, but my gaze slid to Dawn who sat by their side. Quiet, and reserved.

Suddenly the guilt came. Oh boy, did it come. Everything that Dawn had confided in me, everything she had gone through. Ashley was behind it all. Ashley was the reason Dawn was the way she was, and I just fucked her under the bleachers.

I felt sick and slimy, like my very skin was crawling. I needed to find a way to make it up to her. When I turned and saw none other than Ashley fucking Harris climbing the bleachers toward us, I thought maybe I'd have my chance.

A quick glance toward Dawn told me everything I needed to know regarding how she felt about Ashley approaching. I tried to slide in front of her, and turned to greet our guest.

"Kieran," she said as she arrived. "Since when do you slum it with the rejects?" She glanced around me.

"Who the feck are you calling a reject?" Callum scoffed.

"Come join us," she offered her hand to me, a glinting look in her eyes, filled with heat. I was about to be sick just thinking of what we did only a few minutes ago. And yet, it felt like a completely different person.

"No, I'm good here," I declared. Her face fell, something resembling pain flashed across her features.

"Well, maybe if you're lucky, little miss sex-tape here will spread her legs for all of you," Ashley seethed, tossing a vicious glance at Dawn, who curled inward again. "Here's hoping she doesn't have the clap."

Nyx was up in a flash, and Nani came to stand beside me, the three of us forming an impenetrable wall between Ashley and Dawn.

"You wanna try that again? Cause I know you didn't just say that," Nyx threatened, and I felt waves of power and anger pour off of them. Luckily, it wasn't as scary when I wasn't the one who the ire was directed toward.

Ashley stuttered, her eyes widening and betraying her calm exterior.

"So, she's got herself a little harem now? How fitting for a slut," Ashley spat.

"Ashley, petal," Callum said, standing from behind me and slowly making his way around our little wall and planting himself just in front of Ashley. She stood her ground, but I could see the fear dancing in her eyes.

"I t'ink you and I both know that ya aren't going to get

what ya want out of this little... tantrum," he flicked his wrist toward her, like he was disgusted by even her presence.

"Screw you, new kid," Ashley chided.

"Not in a million years, love. Insecure slag is not my type." he jabbed. Salem snickered behind us, and I turned to see she had slid up beside Dawn and had her arm draped protectively around her.

"I think you better be going now," Nani said.

"Don't hurt yourself on the way down," Nyx added, with all the charm of a razor blade.

"Seriously?" Ashley asked, popping a hip and moving her eyes to land on me. My heart rate sped under her knowing gaze. She could tell everyone everything right now.

"Yeah, Oh, and tell Brett, I said hello," I said, hoping it had the desired effect and that she'd stay quiet about our little secret rendezvous. As if Brett didn't already know.

"I'm not going anywhere," she asserted.

"Oh, I t'ink you are," Callum began, stepping up onto the seat of the bleacher between them so he could look her down the barrel of his nose. "I t'ink you're goin' to turn the hell around, and leave Dawn alone. Aren't ya?" He asked, leaving little to no room for argument.

"But-" Ashley stuttered, leaning back from the imposing figure that was Callum Farroway.

"No buts, Miss Harris. That is exactly what's goin' to happen. You *will* leave Dawn Price alone, do you hear me?"

I watched Ashley's body tense under his commanding scrutiny. She didn't exactly shy away, but there was actual fear in her eyes.

"Fine, whatever," she finally said, breaking the tension. "You're a bunch of freaks."

"Do ya promise?" Callum asked, his gaze more intense than I'd ever seen it. Ashley glared back as if he had grown a second head. "I said... Do ya promise?" He demanded again, stronger this time.

"Jesus Christ, yes, ok? I promise. I'll leave your little porn star alone," she relented, fixing the crown that sat atop her head.

Nyx lunged toward her, in a threatening taunt and Ashley quickly scurried down the bleachers away from us. My shoulders relaxed for the first time, and I quickly looked over at Dawn. Her legs were pulled up on the bleachers and she was hugging her knees tight. Damnit.

"You okay?" Nyx asked, sliding in beside Dawn and sliding their arm around her waist. Dawn relaxed between the tandem hold of Salem and Nyx.

"That was intense," I whispered to Callum when he had finally broken his eye contact with Ashley and turned around.

"That was long overdue, is what it was," he replied. I nodded in agreement.

"You think it'll work? That she'll leave Dawn alone?" I asked, glancing over at my new friend who was slowly coming back to herself in the embraces of the people who cared about her.

A mischievous smile spread across Callum's face, a wicked sort of smile that felt just as much a warning as it did a threat. "If she knows what's good for her."

"So, there goes our invitation to her afterparty," Salem said.

"What do we do if we can't be there to stop it?" Nyx asked. Everyone's eyes turned toward me. Ah, yes, the drug expert with the plan. I wracked my brain. I mean, it was bound to be a huge party, maybe she wouldn't notice we were there?

"We could always crash," I offered with a shrug. "She

wasn't going to want us there to begin with anyway, now it's just a little more... explicit?"

"You could probably screw yourself into an invitation," Nyx said. "We saw how she looked at you."

I felt my face flush, but not with embarrassment, but guilt.

"Not an option," I quickly retorted, trying to shift the subject. A small chime drew my focus, and Dawn slipped her phone from her bag to check it. I watched her face fall in real time. Her already pale skin paled visibly and her shoulders hunched over as she read whatever it was on the screen.

"What is it, Dawn?" I asked. She quickly locked the screen and held it against her stomach.

"Nothing," she lied, unconvincingly.

"Dawn, did someone say something to you?" I probed again, feeling anger building with each passing second.

"Just drop it," she urged, and I wanted to respect her wishes, I really did. But I knew something was off, and damn, if I didn't feel responsible for her safety now.

"Dawn," Callum said, sitting in front of her and reaching for her hands. "We're here for you."

Dawn's eyes flicked around the group, all of us, patiently waiting to protect her. There might have been a smile on her lips for the briefest of moments.

"Ashley, just sent me a message," Dawn said, lifting her phone and unlocking it. Turning it for all of us to see.

It was a direct message on some app, and there was a photo of a girl about to eat a hot dog, but there were about 10 dogs in one bun. The text beneath read, 'I'd be jealous if I was a slut like you.'

That's not even fucking clever. Actually, it sounds like she's just jealous.

But clever or not, it was vile. I was furious, and Nyx was too if their clenched fists were any indication. I saw Salem roll her eyes and scoff while Nani murmured something in a different language under their breath. But Callum... Callum wasn't furious, or showing any attempt to be comforting. Instead, I saw that same wicked smile grace his lips almost, excitedly?

Without moving his body, he turned his head toward the dance floor. I followed his gaze, landing on Ashley as she strode smugly across the floor, her heels clicking against the gym floor with each proud step. She was heading toward her friends who were clustered around the refreshment table, their faces bright with excitement. Then, something shifted. It happened in an instant, like all her balance was lost, and her feet slipped out from under her.

Ashley's heel wobbled, and her expression flashed with surprise as she stumbled forward, her arms flailing for balance. But it was too late. She tumbled forward, crashing into the refreshment table with a sickening thud. The punch bowl wobbled, teetering on the edge before tipping over, drenching her with a tidal wave of sticky, crimson punch. The liquid soaked her dress, cascading down her shoulders and chest, but the worst was still to come.

As she fell, the bowl shattered, and a sharp shard of glass caught the side of her forehead. Blood immediately began to trickle down her face, mixing with the punch in a disturbing, dark red streak. She sat there, dazed and humiliated, blinking as if trying to process what had just happened. Her friends gasped and rushed forward, but the damage was done. There Ashley Harris sat, vulnerable in a way no one had ever seen her before.

People rushed forward to help, but I stood frozen, watching with amused attention. My eyes flicked over toward Callum, who unlike the rest of us, didn't seem shocked, or surprised, but instead shrugged nonchalantly.

"Oh no, poor Ashley," he said, with alarming levels of sarcasm lacing his tone.

"I got an idea," Nani said, bursting to their feet and then sprinted down the bleachers toward the chaos.

"What the hell are they doing?" Salem asked and I wish I had an answer, but all I could do was watch as students and chaperones alike flocked around the sobbing and bleeding Ashley, while Nani slid in.

The rest of us remained in our spots, unable to tear our eyes from the scene as Nani ceremoniously exclaimed something to the teachers present. They reached inside their pocket and pulled something out. I couldn't make it out from all the way up here, but with little protestation from anyone involved, they applied whatever it was in their pocket to the gushing wound on Ashley's forehead.

"Holy shit," Nyx muttered, a hint of amusement in their tone.

"Is that..." Salem asked.

"Oh my gods, it is..." Callum said, sitting back with a shit-eating grin.

"Nani just closed Ashley's wound with super glue," I filled in the blanks, a mixture of humor and dumbfoundedness in my voice.

"They did what?" Dawn shouted, her tone was one of confusion, but the vindication in her eyes gave her away.

We watched for a few minutes as Nani, in feigned attempts to make things better, made things so much worse. They pressed a napkin against the wound which was now stuck to the drying glue. I had to place a hand over my mouth to avoid laughing out loud.

When the paramedics arrived, for the second time this week, I scanned their faces to see if I knew any of them, but they weren't any of the old regulars. Nani rattled off something to them before they raised Ashley onto the gurney and wheeled her away. The music had long since stopped and the dance was all but ruined as Nani made their way back to us.

We all sat in silent anticipation as they climbed the bleachers. "What?" Nani asked as they noticed our eager faces.

"Super glue, Ka'Ana?" I teased, letting the humor I was trying to stifle pour out.

"It's an old technique, but effective. She stopped bleeding, didn't she?" Nani responded with a glint in their eyes.

"And that had nothing to do with the fact that gashes closed by glue are more likely to scar horribly, right?" Nyx prompted in a voice entirely devoid of anger, and instead filled with a wicked glee. Damn. All it took was some super-glue and the blood of an enemy. Wish I had known that a few days ago.

"I have no idea what you are talking about," they offered with a smirk.

"Dr. Nani Ka'Ana, MD," Callum teased and Nani smiled back.

"Maybe our problem is solved then," Dawn said, and we all turned to look at her. She was sitting up straighter, a little lighter, her eyes a little less hollow. "The party. She can't exactly host when she's at the hospital."

It was a good point, but that felt too easy. Drug dealers found a way to move product when they needed to, one way or another. "Actually, that might make things more complicated. If they had a plan, and now that plan is out the window, they might improvise. And we aren't really equipped to combat improvisation," I lamented, annoyed that I needed to ruin this brief moment of hope.

"Ok, so we need them to still have the party then," Salem said, and I nodded.

"We need them where we want them," I agreed.

"Give me five minutes," Salem said before standing up and sauntering down the bleachers, her perfect hips swaying.

"Do you think it'll work?" Dawn asked.

"If anyone can convince someone to t'row a party, I have a feeling it's Salem Bridges," Callum responded with a coy smile.

"Weird, wasn't it?" I mused quietly so only Callum could hear me. "You know, Ashley falling and everything."

Their eyes twinkled with a golden glint. "Oh, definitely. The weirdest," he confirmed.

I ignored the nagging feeling in my chest telling me to probe deeper and casted my glance over the gymnasium toward Brett. He didn't leave with Ashley, some fucking boyfriend he is, instead he stood around with some of the other football players and cheerleaders as they gossiped about what had just happened.

His eyes found mine then and while there was heat in his gaze, all I felt was a cold chill of warning spread down my back. Brett locked eyes with me like a man who was looking at everything he ever desired, and yet, I could only see danger. Like an aura, or a cloud around him. A dark shadowed frame dancing around his body, like a blanket of death or fear. I wasn't sure which was more accurate. But something in the way he held himself felt treacherous. Dangerous.

"Salem's coming back," Dawn said, moving down the bleachers to meet her. I followed the group barely managing to pull my gaze from Brett in doing so.

"Rhonda's hosting," Salem confirmed as we met up with her. "Well, she's hosting at Ashley's house, because and I quote 'she'd still want us to have fun, plus I have a key.'" Salem did her very best Rhonda impression, hair flip and all.

"Well done, you minx," Callum said, sliding into Salem's side and wrapping an arm around her waist.

"So, the party is on," Dawn whispered, the weight of our next stop really sinking down on all of us.

"And I guess we don't have to worry about an invitation anymore," Nani chimed in, excitedly.

I looked around at this odd, mismatched group of people who, by all logic, shouldn't belong together. And yet, somehow, it felt like we fit just right. Whatever came next was going to be rough, but I couldn't help feeling a flicker of hope. For the first time, the idea of real friends, people who might actually stick around, was something I craved. But that craving came with a risk... the chance I could lose them. And I wasn't sure what scared me more, the thought of holding onto them... or the fear of watching them disappear. Just like everybody else.

CHAPTER 11

I LOVE THE SMELL OF SUPERNATURAL IN THE MORNING..OR UH.. MIDDLE OF THE NIGHT?

ASHLEY'S HOUSE was exactly as I'd pictured it. Annoyingly affluent, gaudy and unnecessary. I knew I wasn't here to 'party' per se, but I didn't think I would be able to live with myself if I didn't break at least one chandelier before leaving tonight. And just as I found the perfect victim hanging glittering in the center of the foyer, I felt Nani's hand press against the small of my back.

I turned toward them, a smile plastered on my lips.

"You're imagining swinging from it right now aren't you?" They teased, tilting their head toward the large crystalline fixture above us.

"Swinging from it... taking a baseball bat to it..." I responded casually. The brief image of causing destruction to Ashley's perfect little life filled my heart with warmth.

"I'd help you," they said, and when my gaze found them again, they were staring up at the chandelier with an almost hungry expression. Like destruction was their drug of choice and they needed a hit.

"Ok, enough flirting," Nyx interjected, stepping forward. "What are we supposed to do?"

Again, their eyes settled on me.

"We should split up, and well...try to buy some drugs," I said. "When you find the dealer, let us know and we can stop them." As little as I trusted my "angel" right now, I knew that he had the capabilities to take care of this if I got him close enough. I could feel it.

"Who's we?" Dawn asked.

"Me, I mean..." I glanced around at them. "I mean, *I* can stop them. Just find the dealer and then tell me," I corrected, unconvincingly. A few pairs of eyes remained suspiciously trained on my face for a moment.

"Come on, then," Callum said, breaking the tension. "Let's go buy some drugs." He said, cheerily. Like he wasn't about to confront a deadly substance that had the power to hurt a lot of people in this house.

Nyx and Dawn split off in a pair, which honestly I was thankful for. Ashley wasn't here, but plenty of her groupies were and Dawn didn't need to be subjected to their torment all alone.

Nani gave a quick salute, then weaved through the crowd into the living room.

Salem planted a saucy kiss on Callum's lips and then disappeared upstairs. I watched as Callum's eyes trailed after her.

"Hey, I um, I'm sorry," I said, drawing his attention.

"For what?" He replied.

"For kissing Salem at the dance, I promise it didn't mean anything. She's attractive and all, but not really my type," I rambled.

He smirked. "She's everyone's type."

"I just, I see how you look at her, and I'm sorry if you felt like I was cutting in," I concluded. He studied my face for a moment.

"You're a good guy, Kieran Andras." He said it like it was a surprise. "Why don't you let anybody see t'at?"

I turned my face away from him, hating the way his gaze felt like an x-ray. "Believe me, I'm not a 'good guy'. I couldn't be, even if I wanted to."

"I don't believe that. Not even for a second" he mused.

"You don't even know me," I tossed back. I wasn't trying to be rude, but I needed his attention off of me.

"Come on," he said, clasping a hand on my shoulder. Together we weaved through the writhing crowd in Ashley's house. I saw Brett out of the corner of my eye, but tried my best to ignore the way his presence made me feel. I kept my ears open, hoping to hear a single mention of drugs, Sickness, or Bryce's name. But so far, nothing. The look on Callum's face when we locked eyes across the kitchen said he had come up just as empty as I had.

I slipped out the patio door and spilled into the back yard. A dozen or so people were lounging on the furniture, sitting around a fire that someone had started. I circled the edge of the group, listening in on their conversations, but again, heard nothing of note.

"I told you, I didn't want you looking at that fucker." I heard an annoyingly familiar voice chide from behind me. I turned over my shoulder to see basic bitch John, he'd swapped out his handyman clothing for a pair of dark jeans and a wrinkled button down. His greasy hair was slicked back, and his hand was clasped around Hannah's upper arm as he glared at her. Her eyes were wide, and her body language was nothing short of terrified.

I was so fucking over this guy.

"Hey there, John," I said, approaching. Doing my best not to look at Hannah and give him any ammunition to use against her.

"What the fuck do you want?" He spat.

"I guess I'm just wondering why you're here," I said. "This is a high school party, and you're like.. Old right?"

Come on old man, hit me. Just give me a fucking reason.

"What the hell'd you say to me?" He said, stepping forward. Dropping his hand from Hannah's arm.

I flicked my eyes to her for the first time, trying my best to indicate that she should get the hell out of here. She took a few tentative steps, but didn't get far enough away for my comfort.

"Is there a particular reason you have this need to control teenage women?" I prodded, again. Come on, asshole. Step away from her.

He played into my trap, stepping even further from Hannah, giving her a clear path to get away from him.

"I should kick your fucking ass," he threatened.

I didn't mean to look away from him, but I locked eyes with Callum from across the lawn and to my relief, he came sauntering up to stand beside me.

"What's all the commotion over here, Oul Fella?" he asked as he arrived.

"None of your damn business," John chided.

"Hannah, dear, where did you get your dress, it's gorgeous," Salem said, walking up to join the fray. Dawn and Nyx stood nearby, their eyes clocking the situation immediately. She slid an arm around Hannah's shoulders and led her away from John. The two took careful steps away until Salem had led her to stand behind Callum and I. We were starting to garner a bit of an audience, so I tossed a few scathing looks at the onlookers.

"Why don't you all go refill your drinks," I offered and when nobody moved, content to stay and gawk, I added forcefully. "Now!"

The onlookers scrambled inside the house leaving only my group, and him.

"You gonna gang up on me, boy?" John asked, puffing his chest to appear less terrified than he was.

"I t'ink it's time for you to go home, Johnny," Callum said, casually.

"This is ridiculous. I was having a conversation with my girlfriend," he tossed back.

"Do all your conversations include berating and putting your hands on her? Because if that's so, I think it's about time you stopped speaking," I warned.

"Hannah, tell these fuckers to back off. Tell 'em that you're fine," he ordered and I hated the way my own spine went rim-rod straight at the commanding tone, as if my body was programmed to respond to demands.

"You are safe with us, Hannah," Salem whispered. "You don't have to say anything if you don't want to."

"I think you should go John," Hannah replied, meekly.

"Hannah, come on, don't be a bitch," he bemoaned, his anger surfacing.

"Don't call her that," Nyx said, entering the situation. They stepped forward, closing the gap between them until they towered over the little man.

"Hannah, we're leaving, let's go," John said, taking a step back from Nyx's orbit.

"I'm not going anywhere with you, John. Not anymore," Hannah replied back, a little stronger. I was thrilled that she had gained enough confidence to say that. And I couldn't wait to get this asshole out of here.

"Salem," I said simply and she knew exactly what I needed, taking Hannah by the arm and leading her inside, away from John.

"You fucking bitch, Don't walk away from me!" John's voice cracked as he called out after her, desperation mingling with fear. The sound barely had time to reach Hannah's ears before Nyx lunged, and in an instant, their hands were around his throat, hoisting him clean off the ground.

Except, holy shit, they weren't hands anymore.

Nyx's fingers had stretched grotesquely, the bones twisting beneath their skin as they elongated into thick, sinewy digits tipped with razor-sharp claws. The claws glinted in the dim light, as they dug into John's neck. Blood welled up around the tips, trickling down the sides of his throat in thin streams, painting his pale skin with the deep red liquid.

Their nails weren't the only thing that had changed, though. Their arms, now corded with muscle, trembled with an unnatural strength, veins bulging like living roots beneath their skin. Their face contorted, features sharpening with a predatory edge. Eyes that were once dark were now glowing like embers, feral and wild, burning with a rage that was fucking inhuman.

A growl, low and guttural, rumbled from deep in their chest as their lips curled back to reveal elongated, razor-edged teeth. Their jaw seemed broader, their cheekbones more pronounced, giving them an animalistic, almost lupine snarl.

They weren't quite an animal, but not entirely human either. They hovered in some kind of nightmarish limbo, a creature half-consumed by their instincts. Patches of dark fur spread across their arms, bristling as their muscles coiled tighter. Their ears, now slightly pointed, twitched as John gagged and kicked feebly in their grasp.

"What the fuck are you..." John whimpered.

I would also like to know the answer to that question.

"Johnny Boy," Callum said, stepping up next to Nyx, as if

they weren't a terrifying Halloween creature in the flesh. "I t'ink you are goin' to leave this party, and never goin' to speak to Hannah again."

I tried to focus on keeping my breathing steady, ignoring the urge to sprint in the complete opposite direction from the display before me.

"Fuck you..." John spat, but Nyx held tighter, cutting off his airway.

"No, no... I t'ink the words you're looking for are 'I promise'..." Callum warned. And there it was again. Those words. Callum demanded them as if they were some kind of contract.

I thought back to the gym, how he elicited a promise from Ashley, how she'd broken it, how she fell...

The consequences of a broken promise.

Holy shit.

"So, Johnny, what'll it be? Either ya promise to never speak to our dear friend Hannah again? Or I let my friend here tear you apart?"

I glanced over at Dawn who looked equally as shocked as I was. Our gazes collided as a glaringly terrifying truth settled around us.

We were not fucking normal teenagers.

None of us.

"Say it, Johnny boy, and Nyx here will put you down," Callum continued to pressure the dangling asshat.

"Fine, you fucking freaks. I promise to leave her the fuck alone, ok? Jesus!" He screamed out, and I'd be surprised if the asshole didn't wet himself.

That same mischievous smile spread across Callum's face and he leaned back, crossing his arms across his chest.

"T'ank you," he said, with a sickly sweet tone that had my whole body on edge.

"Nyx," Callum said. But Nyx didn't move, their hands held John's throat tight. "Nyx, you can let him go now."

Still Nyx held on, their growls intensified. John's eyes widened in fear. "Nyx, let him go," Callum said, stepping forward cautiously. His voice trembled just enough to betray his nerves, but he kept moving closer. "This isn't you. Just... let him down, okay?"

Nyx didn't respond, their glowing eyes locked on John like a predator savoring the kill. The guttural growl escaping their throat was a warning, primal and chilling.

"Nyx!" Callum tried again, this time with more urgency, his hands hovering over John's shoulders as if preparing to pull him away. "You don't have to hurt him."

But they didn't flinch, didn't even acknowledge him. It was like Nyx had vanished, consumed by the creature that now held John in its grip.

John sputtered, clawing at the massive hands around his neck. Callum swallowed hard, his pulse quickening as he reached out, fingers brushing against John's shirt in a desperate attempt to pull him free. The moment his hand made contact, Nyx snapped their head toward him, baring sharp, glistening teeth in a snarl that froze him in place.

I took a shaky step back, my heart hammering against my ribs.

"Okay, okay, we'll figure this out. Just—" Callum whispered.

Suddenly, the back door slammed open.

"You all better come inside. Now!" Nani's voice cut through the tension like a blade, sharp and urgent as they sprinted forward toward us.

The interruption was enough to make Nyx's head snap in their direction, their eyes still glowing with feral intensity.

They tensed, a low growl rumbling deep in their chest as if sizing up a new threat.

"Wait, Nyx, don't!" I shouted, but it was too late.

Nyx lunged, swiping their claws toward Nani with terrifying speed. The blow caught Nani across the arm and chest, slicing through their shirt and leaving crimson streaks in its wake. Nani staggered back, clutching at the wounds with a sharp intake of breath. John took that moment to stumble out of Nyx's reach.

The moment their claws made contact with Nani, it was like a switch had been flipped. Nyx froze, their glowing eyes dimming as the growl in their throat faltered. The sharpness in their features softened, the fur along their arms receded like smoke being pulled back into a bottle. Their hands trembled, shrinking back to more human-like proportions, claws retracting into bloodied fingers.

"W-what...?" Nyx whispered, their voice cracked and hoarse as they stared at their hands, now slick with Nani's blood.

Nani leaned against the house, wincing but still standing. "What the hell was that?" they muttered, their tone a mix of pain and shock.

I wanted to answer, but I wasn't sure how to. I glanced over at Callum, his attention fixed on Nyx. Their wild, feral energy was gone, replaced by a haunted expression as they took a shaky step back. "I didn't mean to..." Nyx murmured, their voice barely audible. Their hands dropped to their sides.

"You fucking psychos!" John screamed back at us as he sprinted away.

I hesitated for a moment, torn between checking on Nyx and helping Nani. Dawn stepped up toward Nyx, unafraid, settling a hand on their arm. I rushed to Nani's side, helping to steady them. "Are you ok?" I asked.

"I've been through worse, I'm fine," they promised, pressing a hand to my cheek as I held them. "We need to get inside. Now."

"What's going on?" I asked.

"It's bad," Nani warned, before taking a steadying breath and leading us all back into the house.

I was prepared to see some fucked up things tonight, but what greeted me the moment I entered the house was worse than I had imagined.

In every direction, I saw my classmates stumbling around, their faces pale, their bodies uncontrollable as the tell-tale signs of a high were present in their eyes and mannerisms.

"Damnit, we missed the distribution," I scolded, mostly myself. We had one fucking job to do here, and now... I didn't have enough naloxone for this entire party. People could die.

"Salem," Dawn said, stepping forward toward Salem who was standing beside Hannah near the kitchen island. Hannah was swaying on her feet, her eyes rolling back in her head. Her voice was soft and full of little giggles. She was high as a damn kite. "Is she ok?"

"When the fuck did she take the drug?" I asked, remembering the meek and frightened girl of about five minutes ago.

"She didn't," Salem confirmed, holding Hannah steady as she nearly toppled over. "She didn't take a damn thing, Kieran. She was standing here crying into my shoulder one minute, and then... she was like this the next." She met my eyes. "They all were fine, Kieran. And then all of a sudden..."

I glanced around the room, scanning the faces of people who were firmly in the tripping balls portion of their journeys. People I never would have expected to take an unknown drug at a party were twirling around with glazed over eyes.

You see it, now, don't you.

My dark angel said, whispering into my mind.

I ignored the chill of warning that came with his voice, and instead I followed the instinct pulling at my mind and my eyes locked on the air vent.

The Sickness was spreading and I had no idea if we could stop it.

CHAPTER 12

OLD FAMILY RECIPES AREN'T FOR THE WEAK

"The vents," I whispered.

"What?" Dawn asked.

"I think they aerosolized it. It's in the air," I concluded, looking around again at the people who were blissfully enjoying their high. Unaware of the crash that was on its way.

"Seriously?" Callum asked. "It's coming t'rough the vents? Should we cover our mouths? Brush our teeth or somethin'?" He was panicking. I looked over at Salem, then back to Nani, who despite being injured, was not exhibiting any signs of being affected. Both of them were inside the house when this happened. We've been inside for a few minutes now too, and none of us were exhibiting signs.

I clenched my jaw, ignoring the insidious pull to breathe it in. The scent teased me, coiling in the air like smoke from a fire I thought I'd already extinguished. It was a sickening promise, whispered directly into the softest, most vulnerable parts of my mind. A devil perched on my shoulder, beckoning me to take just one breath and let my next high sink into my bones.

My hand twitched toward my pocket where the chip sat, a cruel weight pressed against my thigh. It burned there, scorching through the fabric, daring me, taunting me. It spoke without words, a mocking presence that seemed to hiss, *"What's the point of fighting? You know where this road ends. Just let it all go."*

The memory of what that oblivion felt like- a deep, numbing abyss- flooded my senses. For years, it had been my refuge, a comforting void where the world, with all its sharp edges and suffocating expectations, simply ceased to exist. In that darkness, there had been no pain. No guilt. Just... nothingness.

And yet, even as the temptation clawed at me, something deeper, quieter stirred in my chest. It wasn't the dark angel, with its smirking demands of power and control. No, this was different. It wasn't loud or taunting. It didn't burn or pull. It didn't beg or tempt.

This strength was mine.

I gripped the edge of the counter, grounding myself as the burning in my pocket grew more insistent. My breaths came shallow and quick, the room blurring at the edges as the temptations grew louder, more persistent.

But I didn't reach for the chip. Instead, I forced my breaths to steady, each inhale pulling me back from the edge. I wasn't the person I used to be. I wasn't the scared, broken kid who thought disappearing into nothingness was the only way to survive.

I was still here. And that meant something.

My grip tightened until my knuckles turned white. "No," I whispered, the single word cutting through the chaos in my mind.

I wasn't destined to succumb to this temptation. I wasn't fated to slip back into the shadows.

I was meant to destroy them.

You will always need me, Kieran. You will never be strong enough without me by your side.

My dark angel promised, but I felt his hesitation, his fear. He knew as well as I did that I was the one who pulled my mind back from the brink just now. Not him.

Me.

You are safe from this Sickness... For now. Stop them before that's no longer the case. I'm counting on you, boy.

Then he slipped away again, hiding in the recesses of my mind once more.

"We won't be affected by it..." I whispered again, fear and wonder lacing every word.

"How do you know that?" Callum panicked, bringing the sleeve of his shirt to his nose and covering it.

"Fuck, I don't know..." I was spiraling. I felt it. This was too much. Too fucking much. "I mean, Dawn's a ghost, Nyx is some kind of classic Hollywood monster. Callum can, like, hurt people with promises? I'm still a little fuzzy on that one to be honest. Salem is connected to a devil, Nani doesn't have a fucking soul, and I have an evil angel living in my mind who likes to control me sometimes. Maybe we're not affected because we're all super-fucking-natural!"

They stared back at me, wide mouthed and shocked.

"What do you mean, I'm connected to a devil?" Salem asked, her eyes narrowing.

"Kieran..." Dawn said, hurt flashing in her eyes. Shit, I really shouldn't have said that.

"To be perfectly clear, I don't hurt people with promises, ok? I hurt people who break their promises. It's a.. Well, that's not important right now," Callum interjected.

"How do you know?" Nani asked. They didn't seem angry, or even shocked by any of my admission. Something told me they weren't asking about the others.

"He told me," I said, pointing to my temple. God, I just admitted to hearing voices that controlled me sometimes. If I were them, I'd probably check me in someplace for observation.

"Ok, we obviously have a lot of shit to unpack," Nyx said, speaking up for the first time since their encounter with Nani. "But first, how are we going to save all these people?"

"How much naloxone do you have?" Dawn asked me.

"Enough for five people," I lamented, looking around the kitchen. There were ten kids in this room alone, in the whole damn house, probably another twenty or thirty.

"We need to call the paramedics," I said. "Now."

Salem nodded, slipping her phone out from her cleavage and dialing, all while keeping a steadying hand around Hannah's waist.

"What do we do in the meantime?" Nyx asked, anxiously.

"We need to get them to throw the fuck up," I said, resolved. "And out of this damn house."

"I'll go shut off the air," Dawn said, moving through the crowd.

"I'll start herding people outside," Nyx vowed.

"We need to stop them from reaching the overdose stage, as quickly as possible. Anyone we can't stop. Call for me," I ordered, loudly.

Nani began tearing through the cabinets of the kitchen. "What are you doing?" I asked.

They looked over their shoulder at me, gripping a comically large tub of applesauce in one hand and a bottle of mustard in the other.

"Old family recipe," they admitted, pouring the contents of the jar into a mixing bowl and I watched only for a moment as they started adding other strange ingredients to the mixture.

I joined Nyx in quickly ushering people out of the house

and into the backyard, our classmates were so malleable and out of it, that it was like herding high cats, but we managed to get a solid portion of them outside and into the fresh air.

"They're on their way," Salem said, rushing toward us. She had helped Hannah sit down on the ground, and she was currently staring up at the stars like they were some mesmerizing light.

Dawn and Callum ushered out the last of the people from inside and joined us on the lawn. "That's all of them," Dawn said.

"We need to get them to throw up," I urged, looking around at the people. Some of them had already stopped smiling, and twirling about and were clutching their heads and chests as the drug took a turn in their system.

We were almost out of time.

"Will that even help?" Salem asked, darting her eyes around at the scene. "If it was aerosolized."

"It's the best shot we got," I said.

"How?" Salem cried.

"Like this," Nani said, sprinting up to us with a massive mixing bowl full of something downright vile in their hands.

"Oh, I did not sign up for this," Salem whined, bouncing on the balls of her feet, before gripping a handful of the secret sauce and joining Nani in feeding it to our classmates.

I walked through the crowd as the others got to work, helping our classmates to expel the poison from their systems as best they could, keeping an eye on their behaviors.

Emma was the first to fall victim. Her body began convulsing as she writhed on the ground. I dropped to my knees before her. Gently moving her to her side and holding her head up.

"We got one," I called out, reaching into my pocket for the first dose of naloxone.

"It's ok, Emma," I whispered as I administered the medicine. "I've got you." I held her still as the medicine worked its way into her bloodstream. Her mouth foamed with that eerie green ooze. Looking at it, I felt the unsettling truth that maybe, like us, this drug wasn't all that 'human' either.

"Kieran!" Dawn called for me, I turned and saw that she had her hands on another classmate's shoulders as he writhed on the ground. Once I was confident that Emma was breathing, I rushed over to where Dawn sat.

"I got him, go check on Emma, please," I ordered, and she was off just as I repeated the process with Randy.

The memory hit me like a tidal wave, threatening to drag me under. The scent of sickness- a nauseating cocktail of applesauce, mustard, sweat, and despair– coiled around me like a noose. I could hear them again, my parents, their labored breaths, the groans of pain they tried to muffle for my sake. The soft, pitiful apologies they whispered when they thought I wasn't listening. It all came flooding back, vivid and unrelenting, like some cruel, twisted film reel on repeat.

I clenched my fists, my nails digging into my palms hard enough to sting.

Focus.

I needed to focus. But the ghosts of my past weren't just whispers now, they were a full-blown cacophony, clawing at the edges of my mind, trying to consume me.

The air thinned until I felt like I was breathing through a straw. My chest tightened, and I pressed a trembling hand against it, trying to force the rising panic back down where it belonged. I couldn't afford this right now. There were people I needed to save. To protect.

A loud cry brought my attention back. "Another one!" Callum called out, and I moved over to them to do the same.

My heart pounded like a drumbeat in my ears, each thud echoing with a singular, desperate thought.

Save them. Save them. Save them.

I squeezed my eyes shut for a split second, forcing myself to push past the memories. My parents' faces lingered there, etched in pain, pleading with me like they had in those moments that I had so often thought to be final. Back then, I could save them, but I couldn't stop them. No matter how hard I'd tried, I was always just a kid drowning in an ocean too big for me to cross.

But now?

I wasn't that kid anymore.

My hands trembled as I administered the third dose of naloxone. The final two sitting heavy in my pocket amongst the dozens of my classmates.

My vision swam as I turned to the next person who needed me, bile rising in my throat as the scent of their fear mingled with the phantom stench of my childhood. My knees felt weak, my chest heavy, but I forced myself to keep going. I had to.

"I've done this before," I muttered under my breath, a mantra to keep myself from crumbling. "I've done this before. I can do it again. I have to."

I helped the one in my arms. Giving them the second to last dose. Their convulsions slowed, their breath coming in more evenly now. I let myself have only a moment to glance around.

Dawn was rubbing Emma's back, while comforting another few classmates who had thrown up and seemed to be regaining consciousness. Nani was feeding their weird mixture to the final remaining classmates who were promptly reacting to the vile mixture while Nyx and Salem helped those who had already been sick sit up and breathe.

Callum was rushing around with water, helping anyone who needed it. I watched the faces of my classmates turn from confusion and pain to fear and worry as their senses returned. But as I glanced around, a horrific unsettling thought occurred.

Where's Brett?

The thought hit me like a punch to the stomach, nearly doubling me over. For a fleeting, paralyzing moment, I felt the weight of it all threaten to crush me. My breath came fast and shallow, my vision tunneling.

"Breathe, dammit," I hissed to myself, dragging in a ragged gulp of air. I didn't have the luxury of breaking down. Not now.

"Has anyone seen Brett?" I asked, standing up.

The others looked around the area, but ultimately shook their heads.

He was here. I saw him. Where the fuck is he? I sprinted toward the patio door, a small burst of relief in my chest when I heard the distant sounds of sirens approaching. But the worry gripping my heart for my...for Brett, washed the relief clear in an instant.

Somehow, I kept moving,

"Brett!" I cried out.

"Hey, we'll find him," Nani said, coming to my side.

I offered them a tight nod, afraid to let my emotions show or I'd never control them again.

"Brett!" I called out, rushing through the downstairs floor, throwing open every door in a feral haze.

"What's going on?" Nyx called from the kitchen.

"We can't find Brett," Nani responded.

"Maybe he left?" Nyx responded.

But that felt too easy. Brett was here. Brett was right over there twenty minutes ago. He had to still be in here.

I sprinted up the stairs, taking them two at a time as Nani followed after me. I tore down the hallways of bedrooms, searching. Finally, I came to the final bedroom at the end of the hall and threw the door open.

My heart stuttered, slamming against my ribs as my gaze locked onto the scene before me.

Brett lay sprawled on the floor at the foot of the bed, his body jerking violently, each convulsion a sharp, unnatural jolt. The effects of The Sickness gripped him mercilessly, twisting him into a heap of helplessness at my feet.

But it wasn't just Brett's condition that froze me in place.

It was the figure at the window.

Tall and impossibly lanky, they stood partially shrouded in shadow, the moonlight streaming in behind them. Their face, or what should have been their face, was hidden beneath a dark green, worn gas mask. The stark, unfeeling lenses of the mask turned toward me, cold and alien, as if peering straight through me.

The room felt unnaturally still for a moment, except for Brett's shuddering breaths and the faint sound of my own pounding heartbeat in my ears. That figure wasn't a witness to the chaos. They were the cause of it.

I wanted to move, to yell, to do something, but my body wouldn't respond. I was locked in place, rooted to the ground.

"Who the hell are you?" Nani asked, stepping forward tentatively. My gaze flicked back and forth between the threat at the window, and the man I could have loved once writhing on the ground.

Then the figure disappeared, slipping through the window like smoke, quiet and expertly.

Nani looked over at me, their eyes torn with indecision.

"Go," I urged. "Go, stop them."

Nani offered me a quick nod before following the figure

out onto the roof with similar ease of movement, damn near taking a nosedive out the open window. I didn't have time to acknowledge the worry the action elicited in my chest.

"Nyx, Nani needs you outside! Roof. Now!" I screamed back behind me not waiting to see if they listened to my instruction before falling to my knees before Brett. I pulled the final dose of naloxone from my pocket and administered it, gripping his head in my lap as angry and fearful tears threatened to spill out of my eyes.

"Come on, Brett," I whispered. "Please, please…"

The sirens were getting closer. They'd be here any minute.

"Just stay alive," I pleaded with the man in my arms.

You can't save everybody, Kieran.

His taunting voice returned, sending a jolt of pain and grief to my heart as I watched Brett struggle against the effects of the drug.

Let him go.

I shook my head, tears falling rapidly from my stinging eyes as I pressed my hands against his chest and started compressions.

Let him go, Kieran. The dark angel demanded.

I didn't dignify his command with an answer, despite the way his voice made my body react in fear. Instead, I continued CPR, anxiously waiting for the dose to work.

I sobbed, as I watched his convulsions slow, but in a tense sort of death-filled way.

"No," I cried out, bringing my lips to his and sharing my air with him.

He's mine now. The eager voice cooed, but I couldn't listen. I kept pressing, kept pumping my air into his mouth. My hands were shaking and my body coiled tightly.

Then finally, he breathed.

I exhaled sharply, relief flooding me.

"Fuck," I cried out, releasing tension in my shoulders I hadn't realized I had been holding.

You disobeyed me again...

I didn't have time or energy to respond, and the relief I felt was too strong to be dampened by his challenge.

"Kieran!" I heard Dawn call for me from the base of the stairs.

"What?" I called back, unwilling or unable to leave Brett's side at the moment.

"Nani and Nyx are chasing after some fella in a gas mask," Callum yelled. "They took Nyx's car, come on! We gotta go help them!"

I looked down at Brett, his eyes still shut, but his breathing came clearer and less labored now.

The sirens grew louder.

"Quickly, or the cops will never let us go!" Dawn exclaimed urgently.

I ran a finger along Brett's cheek, a silent message, a good-bye. Then stood and sprinted down the stairs to meet the others.

"Come on, we gotta go!" Callum yelled, dashing out the front door and climbing onto his pale green Vespa. Salem slid on behind him and they jetted off. Dawn and I quickly climbed into the junk storm, and tore out of Ashley's neighborhood, just as the sirens began to arrive on the scene.

I hope we did enough. I hope we saved them all.

I hope we're strong enough to end this for good.

CHAPTER 13

REMEMBER THAT TIME WE DROVE STRAIGHT INTO THE APOCALYPSE?

FOR A FEW PAIN and tension-filled moments there was silence in the car aside from the roaring sound of the engine as we sped down the desert highway. Nani had sent a message to a group chat (apparently, I was a part of a group chat now) telling us to head West out of town, so I did.

My mind drifted back to my less than tactful admission. Revealing secrets that weren't mine to reveal. The guilt of that was sinking into me now that I was able to think about it in the silence.

"I'm sorry, I told everyone," I whispered, feeling the weight of my carelessness heavy in my heart.

"It's ok," Dawn replied quietly.

"No, it's not. That was your secret to tell, and I shouldn't have taken that from you," I admitted.

"Nani already knew, kinda, I think," she admitted. "We never really talked about it, but I think... um," she cleared her throat. "I think when you've died, you can kinda tell when others have too."

My eyes widened, and I gripped the wheel tighter.

"Nani..." I whispered.

She nodded.

"I don't know much, and I can tell they're not...Quite like me. But death is kind of like a perfume, right? You don't know when they put it on, or where they bought it, but you can smell it."

I let that analogy sink in.

"Can you tell if.. I mean.. um .. did I? Do I.. um, smell?"

I never felt myself cross over, I didn't disappear into some big light. I think my dark angel got to me before I slipped away... But I have never been sure. Especially now that I know there are ways to return after death has claimed you.

"You're actually um, kinda hard to figure out," Dawn started. "To use the same analogy, I don't think you ever applied the perfume yourself, but you've definitely hugged someone who has."

I tried to process that. I wasn't dead, but I was close enough to it to have the stench of it remain. Was that a good thing?

Who was it that I held close enough to steal their stench of death?

Dawn?

Nani?

My dark angel?

Silence filled the car again as we crossed out of city limits and plunged into the darkness of the desert heading West.

"Well, I flirt with everything else, might as well flirt with death too," I teased, trying my best to cover up the feeling of adriftness bubbling up.

"Was Brett ok?" Dawn asked after a beat.

"I don't know," I responded.

"Do you think we did enough to save them?" She asked again.

"I don't know," I repeated.

"We did everything we could," Dawn promised.

I nodded, not trusting my voice to remain steady. I turned my brights on, and pressed down on the gas a little more, letting the car speed through the open roads.

"Nani says to head toward Cave Creek Park," she offered, checking the phone that buzzed in her lap. I nodded again, knowing exactly where that was.

"Was it hard?" She chimed in again, filling the silence. "Being around all that, again."

I thought back to the moment I almost tossed away my goals and breathed it in. Before, of course, knowing that it wouldn't have affected me either way.

"Yeah, Dawn," I admitted. "It was hard."

She placed a comforting hand against my shoulder and I leaned into the touch for a moment, letting her presence act as a balm to the searing wound that this evening had ripped wide open. A wound that I had long since considered healed.

"You've been sober for a while now, right?" She asked.

"A year," I replied.

"That's really amazing, Kieran," she said. I nodded, but it felt hollow. I slipped a hand into my pocket, carefully pulling the chip from its resting place and handed it to her.

She held it in the palm of her hand, running a careful finger along the embossed wording.

"I think I'm only sober because of him," I admitted quietly, the words tasting bitter as they left my mouth.

Dawn turned her head toward me, her gaze soft but steady, waiting for me to continue.

"The dark angel in my head," I clarified, the weight of it pressing down on my chest. "He's the one who saved me, the one who pulled me back from the brink of death. The one who gave me something else to work toward in life. He's the only reason I even have that fucking chip," I seethed, the heat rising in my voice. "I didn't earn it. It's not even mine."

Dawn reached out, plucking the chip from her palm with an almost careless ease. She held it up between her thumb and forefinger, turning it slowly, letting the light catch the small ridges and lettering.

"I don't see his name on it," she mused, her tone almost playful.

"My name's not on it either," I shot back, my voice taut with a thin layer of forced humor.

"You know what I meant," she said, a gentle chide laced in her words.

I looked away, my eyes fixing on some faraway point that wasn't really there. "How can sobriety even count," I murmured, "when I wasn't doing it for me?"

The question had been gnawing at the edges of my mind for weeks now, a quiet rot I couldn't seem to cut away. It wasn't just the dark angel's voice that plagued me anymore, it was my own. The doubt whispered in the quiet hours when no one else was around. How could I take pride in something I didn't even own? How could I wear sobriety like a badge of honor when the driving force behind it was someone else?

Dawn's voice cut through the haze, pulling me back to the room. "People all over the world get sober for someone else," she said simply, her words deliberate. "A partner, a child, a loved one. But that doesn't make the accomplishment any less yours."

Her words hung in the air for a moment, a lifeline I wasn't sure I deserved to take hold of.

"No matter what motivated you, you're the one who stopped," she continued, her voice growing firmer. "You're the one who fought. You're the one who chose to stay clean every single day, even when it felt impossible. It's not about who or what started you down the path, it's about who's walking it. And that's you, Kieran."

I wanted to believe her. I wanted to take those words and let them patch the cracks in my foundation. But the doubt remained, lurking in the shadows, whispering that none of it was real. That without him, the angel, the devil, whatever the hell he was, I'd crumble.

Still, I found myself gripping the steering wheel tighter, grounding myself in her presence, in her belief in me, even if I couldn't find it within myself. Maybe someday I'd believe it too. But for now, all I could do was nod, silently, and try to keep the whispers at bay.

Dawn leaned over from the passenger seat, her fingers brushing against mine, begging my tense hold to ease so she could place the chip in my palm. Her touch was deliberate, gentle, like she knew this wasn't just an object to me, it was a lifeline, a weight, a reminder.

The small piece of plastic and metal felt heavier than it should have, like it was carrying the weight of my entire past in its etched surface. The car hummed beneath us, the engine filling the silence as I stared at the chip resting in my hand.

"Take it," she said softly, her voice cutting through the quiet tension between us.

I swallowed hard and nodded, closing my fingers around it. My grip was tight, almost desperate, like I was afraid it would slip through my grasp if I didn't hold it with everything I had.

As I drove, I glanced at it again, just a quick flick of my eyes before focusing back on the road. The chip caught the faint glow of the moonlight, reflecting the months I'd fought to earn it. Months I wasn't sure were truly mine to claim.

Dawn shifted in her seat, her posture relaxed. She didn't

push. Instead, she gave me space to wrestle with it, like she knew this battle was mine alone to fight.

With a shaky breath, I slid the chip back into my pocket, feeling its edges press against my thigh. It was warm from her hand, the heat lingering like an echo of her encouragement.

"You're going to be okay, you know," she said, her voice calm but certain.

I didn't respond right away. The chip was safe in my pocket now, out of sight but certainly not out of mind. My fingers twitched on the steering wheel, gripping it tighter as I felt the weight settle back into place- not just the chip, but everything it represented.

"Yeah," I said finally, though the word felt more like a question than a statement.

Dawn didn't argue. She just turned to look out the window, her quiet presence steady and reassuring.

The road stretched out before us, the headlights cutting through the darkness. I pressed my foot on the gas, the car surging forward, and for a moment, I let myself believe that maybe I could keep going too.

Dawn's phone rang, echoing in the quiet of the car. She drew her hand back from my arm and answered it on speaker.

"Everybody here?" Nani asked through the phone.

A loud rushing sound could be heard, sounded like we were in some kind of air tunnel.

"Yeah! But speak up, will ya?!" Callum yelled into his phone. Ah. Right. He was on the Vespa.

"We're hot on their trail. They're headed into Cave Creek Park," Nyx grumbled, angrily. "Almost lost us a few times."

"What are they doing at the park?!" Callum yelled over the wind to respond.

"Nothing good, I bet," I added.

"What?" I heard Salem yell.

"They said the person is headed to the park!" Callum answered her loudly, filling her in on the call.

"Nobody approaches them alone, ok?" I interject. "Wait for backup," I add, mostly for Nani's sake.

"Fine, but hurry your asses, we're almost there." With that, Nani hung up and we were plunged once again into silence.

"What are we going to do when we get there, Kieran?" Dawn asked, timidly. I wish I had an answer for her, but I honestly didn't.

"Whatever we have to," I vowed, because even without a plan, I knew that much to be true. I would do whatever I needed to in order to keep this Sickness from spreading.

"We're here," Dawn said as I pulled into the parking lot around the same time as Callum and Salem sped in. Nyx and Nani were up ahead on foot, running down the trail after a shadowed figure.

I barely had time to put the car in park before we were out of the car and sprinting after them, up and up and up. Through the winding paths and climbing high into the night sky. My heart was pounding against my ribcage, my breath coming in ragged spurts. I was deeply regretting wearing dress pants right about now.

Four days ago, if you would have told me I'd be sprinting after someone wearing a gas mask who drugged an entire party of high schoolers with a bunch of supernatural teenagers...I would have called you crazy.

I caught up to Callum pretty quickly, but Nyx and Nani, with whatever superhuman animalistic shit they had going on, were clearly ahead, hot on the figures trail. We chased them through the trails for a few minutes, my heart was raging against my chest and my body was screaming at the exertion, but we couldn't stop. We needed to end this Sickness before it could hurt someone who can't come back from it.

We made it to the top of the cliff, the edge jagged and uneven, dropping off into a stretch of endless desert. The night sky was alive with stars, their light mixing with the glow of the moon just enough to make the entrance of a cave visible up ahead. Nyx and Nani were already there, standing at the mouth of it. Their shoulders were tight, their bodies stiff, like they were waiting for something, or bracing for it. I slowed as I came up behind them, a knot of tension twisting in my gut.

"They went in there," Nyx seethed.

"I made them stop and wait for backup," Nani interjected. "They weren't happy, but I pulled the 'you just tried to turn me into ceviche' card, and it worked." They shrugged. My eyes dropped to their chest, no longer bleeding, but marred with the remnants of the wound Nyx had inflicted.

Callum, Dawn, and Salem came barreling up the path, skidding to a stop as they reached us. They doubled over, hands on their knees, gulping down air like they'd just run a marathon. Their heavy breathing filled the silence, their exhaustion written all over their faces.

"So, what's the game plan here?" Callum asked through ragged breaths.

"Stop the Sickness from spreading," I answered.

"Gee, t'ank you! I had no idea that's what we were doing here!" Callum responded sarcastically. "I meant, like... How?"

"I don't know," I said, staring at the mouth of the cave knowing that once we stepped foot inside, things would never be the same.

I stepped forward, turning to face the group, putting the cave's entrance at my back. "There is a chance that whoever ran in there isn't alone. And an even stronger chance that they've got more of that shit in there. We weren't affected at the party, but we can't bank on that happening again." I looked around at their faces, each a mask of anger and fear. "Things might get violent..." I started, my voice barely above a whisper. It felt like the world was holding its breath, waiting for me to continue. This was it, the moment of truth. The one point in time where everything would shift. From here on out, every decision, every action, everything we are, would be shaped by what we chose in this very moment.

Would we hurt them?

Would we *kill* them?

The questions echoed in my mind like a chant I couldn't shake.

How far were we willing to go to stop them?

How monstrous were we willing to become?

Would we cross that line, the one that tied us to what was left of our collective humanity? Or would we step over it, letting ourselves go to the feral nature under the surface?

I swallowed, a tight knot forming in my throat. I had to be ready for whatever came next. But the fear was thick and consuming. Would I be able to live with what came after? Would any of us?

"You need to decide now how far you're willing to go," I urged them, watching as realization flashed on their faces. "If we need to fight our way out of there, we need to be prepared for things to go wrong."

"You think we might have to hurt them?" Salem asked, paling.

"He's saying we might have to kill them," Dawn answered, her voice quiet, but even. Salem inhaled sharply, but didn't respond.

"Our goal is to stop them and bring them to the authorities," Nyx said. "Everyone agree on that?"

We all nodded.

"But, if they won't go.." Nani prompted. "If they try to hurt us... or anyone else..."

Silence hung heavily in the air, thick and suffocating. The kind of silence that's too loud, too full of meaning. And in that silence, something shifted within each of us.

We didn't need words. The decision had already been made, unspoken but undeniable. This was suddenly so much more than teenagers with monstrous powers. It was about something deeper, darker, a line we were about to cross that couldn't be uncrossed.

Our eyes met, one by one, around the circle. No words needed to pass between us. The look in each pair of eyes spoke volumes. It was understanding. We weren't just kids who had been thrown into chaos. We were something else now. We were choosing to embrace the darkness, to step into it fully, to wield it as our own.

And then, in that stillness, the agreement was made. A pact, sealed in the quiet of the moment. No one objected, no one hesitated. We all knew the cost of what we were about to do. And there was no turning back now. We were going to cross that threshold. And once we did, there was no returning to the innocence of what we had been before.

Without another word, I turned on my heel and stepped into the cave. Together we were going to stop The Sickness from spreading.

Even if it cost us our humanity.

CHAPTER 14

IF SOMEONE WEARING A GAS MASKS ASKS YOU TO JOIN A CULT, YOU SHOULD PROBABLY SAY NO

THE CAVE HAD A VERY unique scent that lingered in the air as we entered. Like tar and chemicals. Thick and suffocating. I tried my best to breathe only when necessary, slowing my panicked shallow breaths as much as possible. We luckily didn't need to worry about light, there were cables and worker lights strung along the walls of the cave, leading us to the heart of the tunnel system. Toward The Sickness and the people who did its bidding.

It was a long walk, too long. Every step we took deeper into the heart of the mountains was a step further from our getaway. My fists clenched at my side, frustrated that I hadn't thought to bring a weapon of some sort. My eyes scanned the ground and walls along our path looking for anything that could be used to protect myself, or someone else, should the need arise.

Just ahead, I saw tall yellow barrels scattered across the ground, some toppled over, their lids tossed haphazardly around them. A small puddle of a dark green and black viscous ooze trailed from the open mouth of the barrels. Careful not to get too close, I stepped in to get a better look. Each barrel bore a label of black square with a symbol I'd never seen before. It was a depiction of an obelisk, and it was like something out of a confusing nightmare. It was tall, jagged, more imposing than elegant. The obelisk's surface was marked by cracks, thin and winding at first, but they spread like veins crawling upward, almost as if the stone was alive and rotting from the inside out.

I shot my companions a questioning look, as if to ask if they recognized the image, but they shook their heads, quietly confirming that they, too, were at a loss as to the symbol's meaning.

We pushed forward, leaving the toppled barrels behind us. Then we heard them. Voices. A chill of dread ran down my spine, making my heart thump against my ribcage. Anticipation clung to every move I made, every step I took. I strained to catch their words, but the distance muddled them. Still, the tones were unmistakable. There were at least three different voices, arguing sharply. Probably more. My stomach twisted. I sent up a quick, silent prayer to whoever might be listening. Whoever hadn't given up on me. Whoever could still hear me behind my dark angel's influence.

Please don't let us be outnumbered.

But from the urgency in their voices, they already knew we were coming. It was no surprise, really. We had chased one of them up the cliff, after all. Stealth wasn't an option anymore. If they were expecting us, better to hit hard and fast than give them time to prepare.

I glanced at Nyx and Nani, who flanked me at the front. Their expressions mirrored my resolve, and with a quick nod, we abandoned caution. Together, we charged forward, our footsteps pounding against the ground, ready to meet whatever was hiding in the shadows of this cave.

We squeezed through a narrow opening in the cave and

spilled into a rounded chamber that stopped me cold. Rows upon rows of yellow barrels filled the space, each bearing the cracked obelisk symbol we'd seen earlier. Worker lights hung overhead, casting a sickly glow on the barrels and the uneven earth-carved walls around us. The air was thick, a toxic blend of tar and chemicals that clung to my throat.

Ahead of us stood five figures, each one clad in green gas masks, standing in a straight line, staring at us as we spilled into the space. The masks obscured their faces entirely, turning them into eerie, faceless shapes against the backdrop of the barrels. They stood motionless, their silence more unnerving than if they'd yelled or rushed at us. My pulse raced, every instinct screaming that we'd just walked into something far worse than we'd imagined.

But it wasn't the barrels or the masked figures that truly made my stomach drop. In the far corner of the chamber, a young blonde man knelt on the ground, his body bound tightly with ropes. His hands were wrenched behind his back, and his ankles tied together, forcing him into an awkward, painful position. A strip of cloth was tied around his mouth, muffling the frantic sounds he was making as he struggled against the restraints.

His wild eyes darted to us, full of desperation and fear, I saw a hint of recognition in his gaze as he surveyed us. He didn't belong here, he looked out of place. My breath hitched. Who was he? Why was he here? And what kind of hell had we just walked into?

"Welcome," one of the masked figures spoke, a muffled sort of sound from beneath the mask.

"Why don't you make this easy for us and step away from the barrels," Nyx growled, their voice tight, every syllable dripping with restrained aggression. I could see it, the barely caged feral energy rippling beneath their skin. They were holding it together for now, but just barely.

One of the masked figures chuckled, the sound muffled and distorted through the respirator. "You don't know what you're doing," they said. Their voice was vaguely familiar, stirring something at the back of my mind. Between the adrenaline roaring in my ears and the distorted sound, I couldn't quite place it. "He doesn't want you to interfere."

"He?" I shot back. "Who the hell is he?"

Another figure stepped forward, their body language unnervingly calm. "He is everything. He is all," they intoned reverently, their voice hollow, robotic.

Oh, great. Cult vibes. Just what we needed. I suppressed an eye roll, even as my grip on the situation felt shakier by the second.

"You know, you really shouldn't have drunk that kool-aid," I taunted.

"What does he want from ya?" Callum asked, stepping up beside me.

"Whatever he needs," the robotic one responded. I scoffed.

"He needs you to kill people?" I pressed, taking a slow, deliberate step forward to keep their focus on me. Meanwhile, Nyx and Nani subtly spread out, their movements quiet, measured, like predators circling prey.

"He needs us to spread his message," another voice cut in sharply, this one with more bite. The familiarity of it hit me like a jolt, snapping something into place in my memory. I knew that voice. The realization clawed its way to the forefront of my mind.

"And what message is that, Bryce?" I taunted, the name slipping out like venom. I watched the figure stiffen, their posture sharpening with tension.

Gotcha.

The figure, Bryce, tilted his head, his movements unnervingly deliberate. He reached up and slowly tugged at the straps of his mask. I could hear the strained creak of the plastic as he worked it free. "You don't understand what you're up against," Bryce said, his voice clearer now, sharper. His face was pale under the dim lights, his eyes sunken but lit with something frenzied, something fanatical.

"Maybe not," I replied, my tone even, masking the chill crawling up my spine. "But I know what I'm looking at. A guy I thought I knew, who's clearly gone off the deep end."

Bryce sneered, his lips curling into a twisted grin. "It's not the deep end, Kieran. It's the truth. And soon, you'll see it too. You all will."

My heart pounded as the room seemed to close in, the shadows around the barrels stretching unnaturally. The others in masks shifted uneasily, as if feeding off Bryce's energy. Nyx's muscles were taut, their fingers twitching, claws threatening to break through. Nani had moved closer to the barrels, their eyes darting between me and Bryce, waiting for an opening.

The tension snapped as Bryce raised a hand and pointed directly at me. "He's been watching you. And he's very interested."

"Yeah, well," I said, forcing a smirk despite the panic clawing at my throat, "tell him I'm flattered, but he's not my type."

Bryce's grin widened. "You won't have a choice."

Nani struck then, using their strength to push over one of the yellow barrels. The barrels slammed onto the ground, the lid flying off and the contents oozed out into a puddle on the ground.

Then all hell broke loose.

Nyx didn't hesitate. With a feral snarl they transformed into the creature I now knew them to be, and slashed at the nearest masked figure. The figure darted out of the way just in time for Nyx's claws to instead cut through the thick plastic of a barrel beside them. The sound of tearing rang out, and black sludge spilled across the floor. It oozed like something alive, acrid fumes rising. Nani followed suit, shouldering into another barrel, toppling it over with a crash as more of the liquid sloshed out.

"Stop them!" Bryce bellowed, his voice sharp with panic.

Salem ducked and weaved through the melee, her focus locked on the blonde boy, but one of the masked figures lunged at her. Salem dodged, grabbing a nearby wrench left among the barrels. She swung it hard, connecting with their side. The figure stumbled, but didn't go down.

"Little help here!" she called out. Callum was already moving, throwing himself between Salem and her attacker. With his fists flying, he forced them back, giving Salem room to start untying the boy's hands.

I circled Bryce, trying to keep his attention on me. "So, what's the endgame here, Bryce? Poison the town? Take over the world?"

Bryce sneered. "It's so much bigger than you could ever comprehend, Andras."

"Yeah, that's what people say when they have no idea who they're fighting for," I quipped, inching closer. My heart hammered, but I kept my tone light, trying to pull him further from the others. Bryce moved with me, his focus narrowing as I intended.

Just then another figure came clashing into my side. We toppled to the ground and, with a grunt, I aimed to get my hands between us and shove them off. They were strong, but I was stronger. My arms extended between us, giving me room to breathe, room to maneuver. I swiped at their face, pulling the mask from its place.

I froze, staring at the dark-haired girl I barely knew from school. She blinked up at me, her face pale, her lips pressed into a tight line. "Sarah Guttierez?" I whispered.

Her expression twisted with shame, and she shoved off of me, grabbing for the nearest weapon, a rusted crowbar. I dodged her swing by rolling out of the way, and quickly hopped back to my feet. She shot a worried glance to Bryce who titled his head in a silent order. She followed, rushing back toward the barrels in hopes to preserve the remaining ones.

"You're going to make a very powerful enemy, Kieran," Bryce taunted, and when my eyes flicked back to him, I saw the glint of the metal weapon in his hand.

Bryce lunged at me, his blade slicing through the air. I stumbled back, barely dodging the attack. My heart thundered in relief too soon. He pivoted with terrifying precision, driving the knife into my side.

A sharp, white-hot pain exploded through my ribs, and I screamed, the sound ripping from my throat before I could stop it. Bryce's smile widened, smug and cruel, as he yanked the blade back. It tore free with a sickening pull, leaving a fresh wave of agony in its wake.

Blood spilled down my side in warm, sticky rivulets, soaking into my shirt as I instinctively clutched the wound. My knees wobbled, the sharp sting making it hard to focus, but I forced myself to stay upright, locking my gaze on Bryce. His expression was all triumph.

Behind Bryce, Nani just narrowly avoided taking a crowbar to the head by catching the swinging arm, their teeth sinking into the flesh of the assailant's forearm, ripping at the skin. The figure let out a blood curdling scream, and I forced the disturbing image of Nani's blood stained mouth away for future Kieran to deal with.

Nyx barreled into another figure who had drawn a weapon of their own, their claws gleaming in the harsh light. They tumbled together, and I think Nyx took a hit. But in their current form they seemed less than affected. Salem was still struggling with the restraints on the boy, who had started screaming through his gag while Callum pushed over a barrel.

The boy let out a sharp cry, his voice cracking as Salem frantically worked on the restraints binding him. My stomach twisted when I glanced over. The Sickness had crept across the floor, reaching his legs. Where the dark, viscous substance touched his skin, it sizzled, smoke curling upward like it was eating him alive. His flesh was reddening, the burn spreading rapidly.

"Don't let it touch you!" Salem shouted, her voice strained and urgent. She winced as the ooze seeped around her high-heeled boots, the chemical stench rising in the air. Her hands moved faster, fighting the restraints with a speed born of desperation.

Finally, the bindings gave way with a snap. Without a second of hesitation, Salem grabbed the boy under his arms and hauled him away from the spreading puddle. He cried out again, his face contorted in pain as she dragged him to safety, her heels slipping slightly on the slick surface.

"Hold on!" she urged, her jaw tight, her gaze darting between the boy and the encroaching Sickness. The sound of sizzling and the acrid burn in the air made my skin crawl.

"You're forgetting one thing, Bryce," I taunted, my voice weak, each word edged with the pain radiating from the knife wound in my side. Blood soaked through my shirt, but I forced myself to stay upright, matching his slow, predatory pacing. We circled each other like predators, the tension snapping between us like a live wire.

My gaze flicked from him to the chaos unfolding around

us. The others were locked in their own battles, bodies twisting and colliding. The Sickness on the ground was spreading, its black, viscous form oozing outward like it had a mind of its own.

It crept closer, relentless and hungry, the dark surface glistening under the harsh warehouse lights. One by one, the masked figures fell to it. Their screams echoed as the substance met their skin, eating away at them with a horrifying sizzle. Smoke rose from the points of contact, the acrid stench thickening the already suffocating air. The sight churned my stomach, but I couldn't look away.

The Sickness wasn't stopping. It crawled across the ground, tendrils stretching, reaching, not toward the barrels where it had spilled, but toward the people I cared about. I clenched my jaw, the panic clawing at my chest, threatening to overtake me. Then it hit me. A quiet, unshakable truth that settled deep in my chest. For so long, I'd convinced myself I was alone. But now, as I looked around at the chaos, at the faces of the people who had stood by me, who had chosen to fight alongside me, something shifted.

I had people in my corner. People I cared about. People worth fighting for.

The thought rooted me, steadying my shaky resolve. This wasn't just about survival anymore. This was about them. About us. And I wasn't about to let Bryce- or anyone else- take that away.

"I *am* a powerful enemy," I said, landing a kick directly to his chest. He flew back, landing in the growing puddle of Sickness behind him. He screamed as the drug claimed him, consuming his body like acid corroding plastic. Quickly, efficiently, painfully. I winced.

Nyx, lost in their frenzied state, didn't even seem to register the damage The Sickness was doing to their legs as they sliced through barrels with their claws. The black substance hissed and sizzled against their fur covered skin, but they kept charging after them like nothing else mattered.

Nani clearly saw it too. Without hesitation, they sprang forward, leaping onto Nyx's back in a desperate attempt to pull them away from the spreading ooze. "Get back! You're hurting yourself!" Nani shouted, clinging tightly.

But Nyx, still consumed by the animalistic rage, bucked wildly, tossing Nani off with a sharp twist of their body. Time seemed to slow as Nani hit the ground hard, landing directly in the thick, bubbling pool of The Sickness.

"No!" The cry tore from my throat before I could stop it, raw and helpless. I nearly rushed forward, but the line of liquid death creeping toward me held me in place. Helpless.

The sound, or maybe the sight of Nani writhing in pain, seemed to snap Nyx out of their fury. Their wild, glassy eyes cleared in an instant. Without a second thought, Nyx lunged back toward Nani, ignoring their own injuries as they grabbed them by the arms and hauled them upright.

"Come on, Nani! Get up!" Nyx's voice was sharp, desperate, as they pulled Nani away from the oozing black mess. Nani winced, their face twisted in agony, but they didn't fight Nyx's grip. Together, they stumbled out of the spreading Sickness, leaving a trail of scorched footprints behind them.

I exhaled a breath I hadn't realized I'd been holding, relief crashing over me like a wave.

There were four barrels left standing, the last of the offending drug, and the remaining masked figure stood guard. Despite the Sickness burning their bodies from the outside in, they held their ground, guarding the barrels with a determination that felt uncomfortably familiar.

Reaching them was impossible. The Sickness stretched too

wide, hissing and bubbling like it had a mind of its own. Trying to cross it would be suicide.

Then, out of the corner of my eye, I saw something impossible. A figure floated through the chaos, gliding above the slick black ooze like it was nothing. Dawn. Dawn was flying.

"Of course," I muttered under my breath, too stunned to do anything else. "Why shouldn't the ghost be able to fly?"

She soared toward the barrels, her expression a mix of determination and desperation. When she reached them, she hovered in front of Sarah, who clung to one of the barrels with shaking hands, her body trembling as the Sickness crawled up her legs.

"Grab my hand!" Dawn shouted, extending it toward Sarah. Her voice cracked, pleading.

Sarah's head snapped up, her tear-streaked face twisting in pain and something darker, something devout. "No," she bit out, her grip on the barrel tightening. "The Sickness must spread."

"You're going to die!" Dawn's voice was sharp, laced with fear. "Think of your sister, think of Mya!"

Sarah's knees buckled, and she dropped lower, the Sickness now licking at her waist. Still, she refused. "He..." she gasped, her words interrupted by a wince as another wave of pain wracked her body. "He will save us all."

The unease I had been feeling reared its ugly head again. Her devotion to this mysterious 'he'. The way she put her own life on the line to carry out his orders. I tried not to think of my dark angel. But I couldn't stop the comparison if I tried.

Dawn's face crumpled, and her voice broke. "Sarah, please!" she begged, tears streaming freely down her cheeks. "You don't have to do this. Let me help you."

But Sarah shook her head weakly, her resolve unyielding.

"This is what I was chosen for," she whispered, her voice fading as The Sickness claimed her inch by agonizing inch.

I couldn't look away. Watching her let herself be consumed was horrifying, and all too familiar. Would I have enough strength to say no if my own dark angel asked me to do the same?

Dawn hovered there, her hand still outstretched, her face a picture of grief and helplessness as Sarah gave herself fully to the dark, viscous tide.

Dawn let out a cry, her chest rising and falling as she composed herself. With a resolute nod, she turned her attention to the last standing barrels. Gripping one, she strained against its weight, her lack of leverage in midair making it an awkward and grueling effort. She managed to tilt one slightly, the viscous black liquid sloshing ominously inside, but it wasn't enough.

Then, the cavern was bathed in an otherworldly golden light. It poured into the space like dawn breaking over a battlefield, soft yet powerful, and for a moment, the chaos around us seemed to pause.

I turned toward the source, my mouth falling open. Callum. He had sprouted honest-to-God fairy wings. Iridescent and shimmering with hues of gold and green, they unfurled from his back like something out of a fever dream.

"Oh sure," I muttered, shaking my head at the absurdity of everything. "This is fine."

Callum took to the air effortlessly, his wings propelling him upward in a graceful arc until he hovered beside Dawn. She shot him a look of disbelief, her brows raised in what I could only describe as exasperated awe. Her mouth fell open as if to ask a question.

"Ah ah ah," he said. "Questions later. Priorities," he replied with a cheeky grin before grabbing hold of a barrel.

Together, they made quick work of the remaining barrels, their combined strength finally toppling the last of them. The Sickness spilled out in thick, oozing waves, its hiss echoing through the cavern like a living, vengeful thing.

Once their task was done, Dawn and Callum flew back toward us, landing on a patch of ground still untouched by the spreading liquid. Dawn's boots barely hit the floor before the growing tide of Sickness crept closer, faster than before, like it was furious at being unleashed.

"We need to move!" Nyx shouted, their gruff voice cutting through the mounting panic.

I didn't need to be told twice. The Sickness was spreading at an alarming rate, swallowing up everything in its path. The cavern groaned ominously, and the air thickened with the stench of decay. If we didn't get out soon, there wouldn't be a way out at all.

We stumbled and limped our way toward the exit, each of us battered in one way or another. My side felt like it was on fire, the knife wound pulsing with every movement, and the blood loss was making my head swim. But adrenaline, a hell of a drug, kept me moving.

Nani had an arm draped around Nyx's shoulders, supporting their weight as the two hobbled forward in uneven steps. Nani winced with every movement, but they pushed on, determination flickering behind their pain.

Ahead of us, Salem had the boy's arm slung over her shoulders, practically dragging him toward the mouth of the cave. They were the first to break into the cool Arizona night, their figures silhouetted against the faint glow of moonlight. Dawn and Callum weren't far behind those two, Callum still glowing faintly, his wings flickering like the dying embers of a fire.

The three of us, the most injured, bringing up the rear

were slower. Every step felt like dragging dead weight, but none of us were willing to stop. Not with The Sickness creeping closer, relentless in its spread. By the time we finally reached the cave's mouth, the others were already there, gasping for breath, their faces streaked with exhaustion and relief.

We spilled out onto the cliff's peak together, collapsing onto the rough ground. The wide, endless expanse of the desert stretched before us, a sea of shadowed sand and rock under the starlit sky. The Sickness and the lives it had claimed were firmly behind us, locked away in that hellish cavern.

For a long, heavy moment, none of us spoke. We just breathed, the cool night air sharp and unforgiving in our lungs.

"We made it," Salem finally said, breaking the silence.

I didn't reply. I couldn't. Instead, I tilted my head back to stare at the stars, my chest heaving as the weight of what we'd done, and what we'd survived, finally hit me.

Dawn hurried over to Nyx, assessing their legs and pulling them into a loving embrace. Nyx pulled back, gripping her face in their hands and kissed her. A relief-filled kiss. I turned my eyes away to give them a moment of privacy.

"Thanks for getting me out of there," the stranger said, looking toward Salem.

"What were you doing there?" she replied.

"Dad said that you were in trouble," the boy shrugged. "Didn't know you had the emo version of the Avengers on your side, though. I probably could have avoided all that."

I furrowed my brow at the stranger. His sandy blonde hair and dark brown eyes were slightly familiar.

"I'm sorry... dad?" Salem asked, her tone laced with confusion.

"Yes..." he replied, with a slight eye roll. "Our father-" he said, gesturing between the two of them, "sent me to help you."

"I don't even know who you are," she whispered. I could see the wheels spinning in her mind.

"I'm Derek," he replied, a bright, charming smile playing on his lips. "Your brother."

"That... I don't have a brother," she murmured, the denial was in her words, but not her tone. I could see her putting together puzzle pieces that I didn't have access to.

"Sure ya do," he said, sliding an arm around her shoulders. "Anyway, I need to be getting back. He'll want to know you're alright." He rubbed his knuckles on Salem's head, the way a sibling would, then stepped away from her, heading toward the path.

"Hold on..." Salem called after him, but he quickly disappeared into the night. She stared after him, confusion and pain painted on her features.

I couldn't stand any longer. My legs buckled and I fell to my knees, looking down at the ground below me I saw the pool of blood. Too much blood.

And the more the adrenaline faded, the more the pain gripped my body.

"Kieran," Dawn exclaimed, rushing over to where I was crumpled on the ground. "Oh no," she whispered as she saw the state of my side. "Guys, we need to get Kieran to a hospital or something."

"Nani too, they're not doing too hot," Nyx replied. That drew my attention. I glanced over at Nani, who was covered head to toe in deep vicious burns. They shook violently, trying to take lungfuls of cool air.

"No hospital," I grunted, despite the pain. "I don't have insurance."

I was barely scraping by, I didn't need to slap thousands of dollars in debt onto my plate. I needed someone who was good with a needle and thread, then I'd be fine. I'd been through worse.

"Kieran," Dawn prompted with worry in her gaze.

I waved Dawn's fear away and crawled over to Nani, my movements sluggish and pained. I knelt beside their head, my trembling hands brushing against the unmarred skin of their face.

"Nani," I whispered, my voice cracking. "You're going to be okay. You are." My throat tightened as tears welled up, stinging my eyes and threatening to spill over.

"Yeah, I am," they murmured, wincing through a weak smile. "Just need... a hard reset."

A soft laugh escaped me despite everything, their humor breaking through the weight crushing my chest. "You need a doctor," I said, my voice firmer now, but still thick with worry.

"So do you," they scolded gently, their voice faint but still managing to carry that stubborn tone I knew too well.

I leaned down, pressing a soft kiss to their lips, my touch as light as I could manage. This kiss was something more. Something deeper. It was a promise. A silent plea for them to hold on, to feel the depth of what I couldn't put into words. Though gentle, it carried every bit of fear, love, and hope I had left in me.

"Do me a favor?" Nani asked as I pulled away.

"Anything," I promised.

"Get me over by the cliff," they finished. My brows furrowed.

"Why?" I asked.

"For the hard reset, Special K. Were you not listening to me?" they teased, weakly. Trying to stand. I pushed through my own searing pain and helped them to their feet.

"What are you doing?"